Enamored with a Broodi

HISTORICAL REGENCY ROMANCE NOVEL

Sally Forbes

Copyright © 2024 by Sally Forbes
All Rights Reserved.
This book may not be reproduced or transmitted in any form without the written permission of the publisher. In no way is it legal to reproduce, duplicate, or transmit any part of this document in either electronic means or in printed format. Recording of this publication is strictly prohibited and any storage of this document is not allowed unless with written permission from the publisher.

Table of Contents

Chapter One...4

Chapter Two 10

Chapter Three..15

Chapter Four..22

Chapter Five...28

Chapter Six...36

Chapter Seven..42

Chapter Eight 49

Chapter Nine..55

Chapter Ten 60

Chapter Eleven...65

Chapter Twelve 71

Chapter Thirteen..77

Chapter Fourteen 84

Chapter Fifteen..91

Chapter Sixteen 102

Chapter Seventeen 107

Chapter Eighteen 114

Chapter Nineteen 120

Chapter Twenty 126

Chapter Twenty-One 131

Chapter Twenty-Two 136

Chapter Twenty-Three..140

Chapter Twenty-Four..145

Chapter Twenty-Five...155

Chapter Twenty-Six...162

Epilogue 169

Chapter One

The winds whipped the ocean waves, causing them to break with even greater fierceness. Temperance paused for a moment, her hand still holding tight to the paintbrush before she swept it across the canvas.

My heart is like the waves. Unsettled and never finding stillness.

Tears came to her eyes and one dripped to her cheek. Hastily, Temperance wiped it away, only for her fingers to trace the scar there.

Shame burned through her and she closed her eyes, swallowing hard as she shook her head to herself. It had been two years since that dreadful day, two years since she had not only been broken in body but also in spirit. Two years since she had felt any sort of happiness.

Blinking back her tears, Temperance took in a long, steadying breath and once more, looked out at the tempestuous waves. The artwork was beginning to take shape, the waves and the shore clearly depicted but yet, she was still not contented with it. There was so much more she had to do, so many fine details she had to paint in. There was the froth of the waves as they crashed against the coastal cliffs, the fury of the wind as it whipped up the sea and the shadows of the gulls as they flew overhead. She wanted to capture all of it. Every single last moment. It was the only way she could forget about her past, the only way she could set aside all of her pain and her sorrow. Focusing solely on her artwork, thinking only about the scene before her, that was the only course she had for a little relief.

"Do come and sit down for a while, my dear."

Temperance turned to see her aunt smiling gently at her from the door of the parlor.

"I have a tea tray set out for us in the drawing room. Will you not come and sit with me for even a few minutes?" Lady Hartford offered Temperance a small, slightly wry smile. "I have received a letter from your mother and she did beg of me to speak of some things with you."

Temperance's stomach twisted. "I have not quite yet finished my painting, Aunt."

"But you will stand there and paint until it is too dark for you to see the scene before you and by that time, it will be too late for tea," came the reply, though Temperance could tell that her aunt was doing her best to encourage her away from what she was doing simply because she wished her to take a little rest, rather than because of the hour. Aunt Matilda had always been very concerned and considerate when it came to Temperance and though she was grateful for that, Temperance wished that, on occasions such as this, she would leave her to paint rather than encourage her to take tea instead. Taking tea would mean conversation and discussion about her present situation and Temperance did not want that.

"Please, Temperance."

The softness of her aunt's voice made Temperance's heart squeeze. "Very well, Aunt."

Lady Matilda smiled. "I thank you. The tea will warm your hands, I am sure. This parlor is rather cold today. I will have a fire set for you and then when you return, the room will be a little warmer."

"By then, I fear that the sky will have darkened and I will not be able to paint."

Her aunt laughed softly. "My dear girl, it is only mid-morning! You will have plenty of time to paint today. I will have the maid set the fire so it is a little warmer for you. Now please, do come and sit down. You need to take a short respite, I am sure."

Temperance followed her aunt through, pausing only for a moment as her aunt instructed a maid to set a fire in the parlor for Temperance's return. Once seated in the drawing room, she accepted the cup of tea from her aunt and settled back a little more into her chair. Her body softened, a few aches in her neck and back becoming a little more prominent and she let out a slow breath.

Perhaps I did need this.

"You said you had a letter from my mother?" Temperance asked, seeing Lady Hartford nod. It was not something that she wished to discuss but, knowing that her aunt wanted to say something to her about it, Temperance considered it was best to bring it to the fore rather than hide it away. "What is it that she wishes you to say to me?"

Her aunt set down her tea cup and then reached for a letter which was sitting quietly on the table beside her. "Do you wish to read it yourself?"

Temperance shook her head. "No, I thank you."

"There is nothing personal within it. But given that she writes a letter to you every sennight, I suppose that there is nothing written within this that she has not already said to you." Her aunt offered her a small, wry smile. "Aside from the grave concern that she is expressing about your continued residence here."

Temperance's eyebrows lifted. "My mother does not wish me to reside here with you any longer? For what purpose?"

Her aunt let out a small sigh. "It is not that she does not want you to reside here, Temperance. It is only that she is concerned about your *absence* from London."

Temperance closed her eyes, her heart dropping low. "She wants me to return to society?"

"Yes, I believe so."

"But why?" Opening her eyes, Temperance shook her head. "There is no purpose in my return to society! It is not as though any gentleman will look at me – will look at my scarred face – and consider me worthy of courtship!" Seeing the way her aunt's gaze darted away, Temperance closed her eyes again. "She wants me to make a match, does she not?"

Lady Hartford nodded just as Temperance opened her eyes. "Yes, I believe that that is her desire for you."

Temperance took a sip of her tea, trying to calm the upset which grew up within her. "My mother is thinking foolishly. I cannot make a good match! It has been two Seasons since I was last in society and it is not as though my face has changed in any way. If anything, despite the doctor's best efforts, my scar remains just as prominent as it has always been."

"That is not so." Lady Hartford smiled encouragingly but Temperance did not even permit it to enter her heart. She knew all too well the long, jagged scar which ran from the side of her eye all the way to her jawline. She saw it every time she glanced at herself in the looking glass. Her lady's maid had, at times, attempted to conceal it by permitting some of Temperance's golden tresses to fall lightly to one side of her face but even that had not hidden it completely. Temperance was certain a return to London and to society would only make her the topic of every conversation and, what was worse, no gentleman would even so much as glance at her for a second time.

"Your sisters are both married and settled," her aunt murmured, gently. "It is only right that your mother should now consider you."

"My sisters both have perfect complexions, Aunt." A seed of bitterness entered into Temperance's heart. Her sisters had cared very little about what had happened to Temperance, seemingly to be nothing but relieved that *they* had been spared such a thing. They had barely spoken to Temperance as she had recovered from the accident and in the two years that Temperance had lived here with her aunt and uncle, neither of them had written to her to see how she fared. The only way Temperance had heard of their marriage was through a letter from her mother. She had not even been invited to their weddings. Evidently, her sisters had not wanted to have their beautiful ceremonies spoiled by her presence.

"You must not let your injury – and the scar which lingers – define who you are. And certainly you must not let yourself believe that every gentleman in London will look at you and see only your scar!" Lady Hartford leaned forward in her chair, a gentle gleam of encouragement in her eye but Temperance only shook her head. "Come now, Temperance," Lady Hartford continued, gently. "You are intelligent, talented – your paintings are beautiful – and you have excellent conversation, poise and elegance. Your heart is compassionate and kind. There is more to you than your outward appearance, is there not? And the right gentleman will see that."

"I do not think I can believe that, Aunt." Temperance sipped her tea so that she could hide her tears from her aunt. In the last two years, she had done nothing but consider what had happened at the time of her accident and, thereafter, considered just how bleak her future might be.

"Do not think that every gentleman is like Edmund, Temperance."

A harsh note entered her aunt's voice and, a little surprised, Temperance blinked back her tears as she looked to the lady. Lady

Hartford was scowling, a shadow flickering over her expression as she looked away from Temperance and to the window instead.

"I fear, Aunt, that most – if not every – gentleman in London is like Edmund," Temperance admitted, in a half whisper. Edmund, the Marquess of Barlington, had been her betrothed at one time. He had declared his devotion to her, had stated how much he adored her and how much joy there was waiting for them and Temperance had believed every word. In fact, she had been swept away by him, overcome with hope and excitement as to what their future as man and wife would be – and then the accident had happened. They had been out riding with some other friends and acquaintances at his estate, when her horse had shied suddenly. Temperance had been thrown from it, pain lacing through her body and her head – and her face also. She had been injured, yes, but those injuries had healed. It was the scars they had left behind which had pushed Edmund away.

Her eyes closed, a slight tremble running through her. The moment Edmund had told her that their engagement had come to an end, she had felt her world shrink. He had not been able to look at her, had not been able to keep her gaze and that had told her everything she had needed to know about him. The gentleman was a coward, yes, but he had broken her heart regardless. Too late, she had realized that there was nothing genuine about his supposed affections. He had been nothing but a fraud, pretending that he felt more than he truly did and she had accepted every word from him as truth.

Darkness had overtaken her, then, and even now, it had not left her. She was torn apart, broken by his betrayal, shunned by the injuries she had endured. Her beauty was marred, her heart shattered and all that had been left for her was to retreat.

"You will not return to London, then? You will not go back to society for the Season?"

Her aunt's quiet question whispered to Temperance and she quickly shook her head, blinking back the tears which returned to her all too quickly.

"I do not think I can, Aunt," she whispered, honestly. "It is already too much for me even to *think* of it."

Lady Hartford smiled and nodded gently. "I understand," she said, softly. "I will write to your mother and tell her that we have spoken of it. That will satisfy her, I am sure."

Temperance managed a slightly wobbly smile but then excused herself to go back to her painting. The room was already a little warmer thanks to the fire which had been lit but Temperance's turbulent emotions were more unsettled than ever. She picked up her paintbrush, ready to begin again, but her vision was quickly blurred with tears. Temperance sniffed and closed her eyes tightly to press them back but they refused to listen and instead, continued to come. Setting her paintbrush down, Temperance dropped her head and let the tears fall. There was still so much pain within her heart, a pain which never seemed to fade or disappear. It was all she could do to bear it.

Chapter Two

"I am certainly *not* disappointed that we did not stay in London this Season, not when I can smell the sea air from here!"

James glanced to his mother and permitted himself a small smile though, inwardly, his heart ached heavier still as the very same scent which brought his mother such comfort brought himself a good deal of trouble.

"It is a wonderful place," his mother continued, speaking as though she were alone in the carriage. "It has been too long since we were able to return here."

James let out a slow breath. "I am sorry it has taken so long," he answered, seeing his mother look to him directly. "There has been much to do since... well, since the sorrows which have broken our hearts."

Lady Calverton reached across and touched his hand. "You know that I do not blame you for your brother's death."

A shake of his head was James' only answer.

"He was not as he ought to be," Lady Calverton continued, her voice wobbling a little as James turned his head to look out of the window, aware of his own emotions rising steadily. "He should have taken on the title with decorum and with a seriousness which he did not possess. I am broken-hearted over his passing but I am not about to pretend that he was everything that he ought to be."

"I should have been here," James muttered, shaking his head. "The Great Adventure was not something I was *required* to take on. It was something I chose to do."

"It is something that many a gentleman takes on, however, and you had every right to go and explore this world, just as you pleased! You were the second born, you were not the one who was to bear any great responsibility. Your father was pleased that you were to go to other countries, just as he himself had done."

"I missed his passing, however," James answered, his heart aching all over again. "And by the time news reached me of the funeral, Simon had already taken on the title and had not even considered the mourning period! I returned home to find him in such a degenerate state, he could not be saved from it. Had I been in England, had I been present at the time of father's passing, I might have been able to do something to protect him from such a path."

Again, his mother reached across to take his hand, though this time, she held on a little longer. James was forced to turn to look at her, seeing the tears glistening in her eyes but also the tightness about her jaw.

"You did nothing wrong in behaving as you did," she said, firmly. "Your brother chose to go to that gambling den. He chose to place a bet with coin he did not have. He chose to take on a foolish fight when he was already heavily in his cups. His death might not have occurred had he not chosen to do all those things but when we consider what happened, we have no choice but to place the guilt solely upon his own shoulders."

James shook his head. "It was such a waste, was it not?"

"The money he threw away?"

Holding his mother's gaze, James' heart turned over in his chest, guilt still rattling around him. "His life, Mama. I mean that he threw away his life because he was chasing pleasure rather than responsibility. I do not think that such a choice was worth it."

A small, sad smile came over his mother's face. "No, it certainly was not. No amount of money is worth one's life. But your brother would not listen. I tried to reason with him but he refused to listen to me. I can promise you that, had you been in England, he would not have listened to you either."

"Ah, but I could have tried," James muttered, closing his eyes and pulling his hand away from his mother's. "That might have assuaged my guilt just a little."

"It is guilt that you do not have to bear," she said, firmly. "Release the burden from your shoulders, my son. We have enough pain to deal with already."

When James opened his eyes, he saw the smile on his mother's face, though he did not understand it.

"You must know how proud I am of you," she said, when James' frown grew heavier. "You are a gentleman who has done nothing but shoulder the responsibility that you were never meant to have. Your brother almost ruined us but you have brought us back to respectability. I know how hard you have worked to regain our fortune. I know how much you have taken on, the decisions you have had to make, the struggle that the last few years have been. But we are now returning to the smaller estate by the shoreline, an estate which we feared we would have to sell, but instead, we are now returning there for a short respite."

"It is to be your Dower house, mother," James reminded her, seeing the smile that spread right across her face, sending light into her eyes. "I would have done anything required of me to keep it for you. I know how much you adore this place."

Lady Calverton pressed his hand tightly one more time, then released it as she sat back up into her seat. "My dear son, you bring joy to my weary heart." She tilted her head. "But you like this place also, do you not? The curl of the waves on the sea, the wind which runs wildly through the trees?"

"The howling gales and the torrential rain?" James added, a little wryly as his mother laughed. "I am not certain that I shall appreciate such things as that."

"Though there are many memories of such things, I know," came the reply as James nodded, his smile fading. "We came here many a time when you and your brother were boys. I have always been fond of it. Besides which, I believe that it is very good for one's health and perhaps now, more than ever, we need to have such a respite!"

James nodded but did not smile, turning his head to look out of the carriage window again. The carriage turned into the long, gravel drive but before it could go any further, James reached up and rapped on the roof.

"I think I shall walk for a short while before I return to the house," he explained, as the door was opened for him. "I have been sitting in this carriage for much too long and require a little fresh air. Will you be quite all right by yourself?"

His mother nodded, not questioning what it was that he desired to do. "I shall be perfectly contented. I intend to take tea in the parlor and look out across the estate towards the sea."

James smiled briefly, nodded and then stepped outside. Giving the driver the instruction to take his mother and all their other belongings to the manor house, he turned and strode away from the carriage, making his way out of the driveway and instead, along the path to the side of the estate. Many a time he and his brother had walked along this path as boys, many a time had they escaped together from whatever his father had been intending for them to do. He knew exactly where it led and, all these years later, the path itself was still intact. It led him through the moorland,

moorland which was damp under his feet, until he came to the top of the cliffs.

It was there that James paused, his hands going to his hips, his face turned to the wind as he looked out across the waves. The spray of the sea blew up towards him, coating his skin but James made no effort to wipe it away. Here, at least, he felt as though the wind were blowing away some of the heaviness which had clung to his soul for the last few years. Here, he did not have to think about his bills, about his income, about the crops and the many debts he had still to pay. Here, he could be free of all of that for a time.

This last year, his stocks had done marvelously well and, thus he had been able to pay off the last of his brother's debts. It meant that he had very little to put into the rest of his business, but it was enough to know that there was nothing else required to be repaid. He had succeeded in keeping the dower house *and* his own estate – albeit in the knowledge that some improvements would soon be required – and that had been a great blessing to his mind. For the first time in some years, he was going to permit himself to do nothing as regarded his estate and business affairs. He was going to take some time to walk through the moors, to walk along the shoreline, to let himself feel a freedom which had evaded him for some time.

I am sorry I did not come back in time to stop you, Simon.

James dropped his head, the guilt which had forever plagued him returning back again with force. It did not matter what his mother had said, it did not matter what she had tried to encourage him with, he still felt responsible for his absence. If he had been present, then Simon might never have fallen as far as he had done – and his death might never have come about. *He* would be the Earl of Calverton and James would have his own position under that but now, James himself had the responsibility to the estate and to his mother. A responsibility that he had never been meant to have.

"But I will do my utmost to keep our name and the family title respectable," he muttered, as the wind chased the words away as soon as they had been spoken. The shame which Simon had brought to them all had been great but James was determined to restore it.

Though that means that I must find a suitable match.

Scowling, James shook his head to himself, turning away as he walked back along the path towards his estate. He had eschewed the thought of making his way to London for the Season. He did not have enough of a fortune to consider matrimony, not as yet, and, were he honest, the thought of stepping back into a society who would still look at him and whisper about all that his brother had done was not a pleasant one. No, for the moment, James would keep his thoughts away from such things. When the time was right, *then* he would force himself back to society but for the moment, his place was here. Here, in the wind and by the waves; a place where he might be free.

Chapter Three

Temperance hummed quietly to herself as she made her way down the familiar path from the estate to the cliffs. Her uncle, Lord Hartford, had taken great care to show her the way when she had first arrived at the estate, telling her that he often found great solace there and thinking that she might find the same.

How right he had been.

She smiled to herself, thinking of her uncle and wondering when he might return from the continent. He had been gone some months now, though his letters assured both herself and her aunt that all was well – and that his interests abroad were doing very well indeed. Both he and her aunt had encouraged her love of sketching, drawing and painting in a way that no-one else ever had, insisting that she purchase whatever she required and with her uncle firm in his resolve that *he* would pay for it. How grateful she was to them both for the love they had shown her, as well as their gentle understanding. It was clear to Temperance that her own parents – her mother especially – did not seem to understand just how much sorrow and pain she still bore from her scar. Her mother's urging to return to London had been difficult for Temperance to hear. Did her mother not realize what society would think of Temperance and her outward appearance? Did she not see that there would be nothing but whispers and rumors flying around the *ton* about her? Was she truly so desperate for Temperance to marry that she would force her back into London society?

She cannot force me, Temperance told herself, aware of the slight trembling which ran through her. *I will not go, no matter how hard she tries.*

A little breathless from the quick walk she had taken, Temperance paused at her favorite spot, catching her breath and looking out towards the sea. She stood at the lowest point of the cliffs, the shore beneath her, though her uncle had warned her never to climb down to the shore from *this* part. Instead, there was a path a little further along the way which Temperance took sometimes. But not today. Smiling to herself, Temperance sat down on a large rock which, she sometimes thought, had been placed there by God himself, knowing that she would one day use it to sit on so she might draw, and took out her paper and pencil.

Her eyes searched the horizon, taking everything in and then, she let herself begin to draw freely. There was a darkness to the sea today which caught her attention. Some parts danced with light as the sunshine bounced from the tops of the waves and the breakers, whereas most of it held a strength of deep color which she could not help but take note of. She sketched quickly and carefully, already eager to return home and begin to paint this very scene. She wanted to remember all of it, wanted to take in every part and thus, she made every single press of her pencil with great care and precision. Her lips pressed tight together as she gave all of her concentration to her sketch, hearing the cry of the wheeling gulls above her head, mixing together with the crash of the waves beneath. The sketch quickly came together and Temperance offered it a small smile. She was pleased with what she had captured, all too aware of how quickly the landscape could change and just how much of it she could miss if she was not hasty enough.

Rising to her feet, Temperance placed her pencil back in her pocket, ready to return to the house and begin painting, only for a sudden gust of wind to snatch the paper from her hand.

"No!" Temperance rushed after her paper, her heart pounding furiously. Already, the sky and the sea had changed and if she were to lose that paper, she would not be able to keep a hold of the scene in her mind for long enough to paint it. The wind teased her, pulling the paper away from her grasping fingers and then letting it fall again, letting it settle on the grass for only a few moments before tugging it away again. Temperance stumbled a little, her mouth going dry as she thought of the paper being pulled into the sea, losing it forever. Her art was her only passion, the only thing which made her heart sing and her spirits lift. Others might say that it was only a sketch but to Temperance, it was of great importance.

"Please!" she cried aloud, as though the wind might listen to her and stop what it was doing. Instead, it ignored her cries, pulling the paper down over the edge of the cliff and down towards the shore. Her heart in her throat, Temperance made her way to the edge, looking down helplessly, watching as the paper dropped lower and lower... only to snag against a piece of driftwood which stuck out from between the rocks and stones which lined the top of the shore.

She hesitated.

The path which led down to the shore was much further along the cliffs and if she were to take that, if she were to make her way there and, thereafter, hurry back towards the paper, then she had very little hope of finding it again. The wind, in all its mischief, would have taken it away from her again and, no doubt, flung it onto the soggy sand or the sea itself and then what would she do?

Temperance swallowed tightly, then began to descend. This was the lowest part of the cliff face but all the same, it was not as though there was a simple path for her to follow. Instead, there were jagged rocks, sometimes hidden by the outcrops of earth and green grass which she stepped onto cautiously. Thereafter, large boulders greeted her, smaller rocks in between them and, once she had climbed over them, smaller stones and even pebbles which slipped beneath her feet.

Temperance let out a gasp of fright as she wheeled back, her arms spread wide, her hands reaching for something – anything to find. There were a few feet of a somewhat steep descent still to make and if she were to fall...

"Ho! You there! Whatever do you think you are doing?"

Temperance started in fright, having never once expected to hear someone else shouting through the wind. She could not even turn her head, ending up falling back and sitting down heavily rather than falling forward. Her body cried out in pain, her skirts putting only a little softness between her skin and the rocks, though she did not let a single sound come out of her mouth.

My sketch!

"Whatever are you doing?" the voice said again – but Temperance ignored it. Rising to her feet, she kept her attention fixed to her sketch. The driftwood still held it fast, though the edges fluttered in the ever-present wind. With urgent feet – but feet which still slipped across the stones and pebbles – Temperance made for it, her worry pushing her into a faster pace than she ought otherwise to have gone. With a cry of relief, she caught up her sketch, holding it fast, only for her feet to slip again. Letting out a cry, she half fell, half ran down the remaining stones to the shore. She did not think she could stop, her eyes wide, the wind whipping at her hair and her skin... and then something solid stopped her.

"Ho, there!"

Her breath ran out of her body as she blinked furiously, only to look to make quite certain that her sketch was safe in her hands. Sagging with relief, Temperance closed her eyes, only to then realize that whatever had stopped her was still very much present.

"Are you quite all right?"

A flare of fright rushed up Temperance's spine and she quickly turned her head away, hiding her scarred cheek from this somewhat imposing gentleman. "Yes, I thank you." Her voice was quiet but she focused on folding her sketch back into her book. "The wind stole something from me and it was imperative I found it again. I was afraid it would be taken to the sea."

"You ought not to have climbed down that way," came the reply and this time, Temperance dared a glance at her unexpected companion. Her stomach twisted, her heart pounding rather furiously as she looked into the gentleman's face and saw the deep frown which settled across his forehead. There was a rather serious expression etched there, his hazel eyes fixed and firm as they looked back at her, dark hair over his forehead though his hat, despite the wind, remained quite steady. Temperance looked away again, taking a step away from him.

"As I have said, I was afraid that it would be taken to the sea and I would have lost it forever," she answered, afraid now that this fellow might be someone nefarious and all too aware that she was standing alone with him on the otherwise deserted beach. "I thank you for your help."

Much to her surprise, the fellow took off his hat and, just as any gentleman of the *ton* might, bowed very low indeed.

"But of course. I am only glad that you did not fall and hurt yourself! I presume whatever you took back from the wind is now safely secured?"

Temperance nodded, making sure to keep her scarred side of her face away from him. "I have. "

"Very good. Then might I escort you back?" He offered her his arm but Temperance quickly shook her head. This fellow, whoever he was, was certainly dressed as a gentleman but that did not mean that he truly was one. She did not know his name and certainly could not guess at his motivation and thus, refrained from accepting his company.

"I am well able to make my way back to my aunt's house alone, I thank you." She took another step back. "I have lived here for a long time and am well acquainted with the path."

"Then I am surprised you did not take it as you came down," he said, not offering her a single hint of a smile. "Did you say that your aunt's house is nearby?"

"I did not but yes, it is," Temperance answered, making another step away from him. "Lord and Lady Hartford?" She lifted her chin, thinking to herself that to mention the name of the Viscount Hartford would mean something to this fellow. Mayhap he would be more cautious in approaching her if he knew that she was highly connected. Much to her surprise, however, the gentleman's expression cleared and he smiled, suddenly.

His expression transformed. Instead of a frown sending shadows into his eyes, there was a brightness there which filled his entire expression. His hazel eyes seemed a good deal more vivid and even his cheeks seemed to fill with a little more color.

"Ah, how wonderful! I am very glad to hear that the Viscount and Lady Hartford are still present here." He bowed suddenly, then stepped closer to her. "Did you say she was your aunt? Then you must tell them both how eager I am to see them again – my mother will be eager for a reunion also! It has been some years since we have been able to return to the manor house here but now that we have come back, I am hopeful that previous connections can be reestablished."

Temperance blinked in surprise, though she still did not turn fully towards him. The moment she did so, Temperance was certain that shock would replace the evident happiness in the gentleman's expression and nothing but mortification would fill her. "My uncle is away on business in the continent," she said slowly, as the gentleman nodded. "My aunt is still at home, however. Might I ask as to whom I should say is eager to speak with her again?"

The gentleman dashed one hand over his forehead. "But of course. Forgive me, I have not yet introduced myself. Goodness, I am not as improper as I appear, I promise you!" He smiled again, then inclined his head one more time. "The Earl of Calverton. My mother is Lady Calverton, and I am certain she will be utterly delighted to see Lady Hartford again. It will mean a great deal to her."

"I – I am glad to hear it." A little uncertain as to what to say, Temperance dropped her head, keeping her gaze on the book of sketches she had in her hand.

"Are you certain I cannot escort you?" he asked, as Temperance quickly shook her head. "The path is rather far away and – "

"I have walked this way many times," Temperance told him, relieved now that she could take her leave of him. "Do excuse me, Lord Calverton. I will, of course, pass on your words of greeting to my aunt."

"And I will tell my mother of Lady Hartford's presence also," came the reply. "A pleasure to meet you, Miss…" A frown flickered across his forehead, stealing his smile away. "I realise now that I do not yet know your title, my lady. Might I ask for it?"

Letting out a slow sigh as urgency pushed her away from him, Temperance forced a small smile. "Lady Temperance, my lord. My father is the Duke of Danfield."

Lord Calverton blinked. "I see."

He did not smile and Temperance flushed hot, despite the chill in the wind. Did he know of what had happened to her? Had her name brought about a flash of understanding as he recalled whom she had once been engaged to?

"I should return now," she murmured, making her way back towards the path which led a winding way up the cliffs. "Do excuse me, Lord Calverton."

"Good afternoon, Lady Temperance."

Temperance scurried away as fast as she dared, without making it appear as though she were hurrying away from him. Her face grew hotter still as she wondered if he were watching her, afraid now that he would be gazing after her with the realization as to why she had hidden her face from him. Making her way to the path, Temperance paused for a moment to catch her breath, all thoughts of her sketch and her upcoming painting now gone from her. That had been a most unexpected meeting and, all of a sudden, she felt herself unsettled and filled with concern rather than the quiet happiness which had filled her as she had sketched. A good deal more slowly now, Temperance made her way up the cliff path, daring a glance back over her shoulder as she climbed.

Lord Calverton was still walking along the shoreline, though away from her rather than coming back towards the path. Feeling a little more secure now, Temperance slowed her steps even more, considering him and their strange introduction. He appeared to be a somewhat serious gentleman given his demeanor and his expression, though that had lifted for a few moments when he had learned who her aunt was.

I do not think that I will be often in his company, she thought to herself, comforted by the thought. *His mother can visit my aunt and I am certain that my presence will not be required.* Nodding to herself, Temperance made her way back along the top of the cliffs towards the house, doing her best to turn her thoughts towards her sketch rather than Lord Calverton. Her breathing still quickened from her ascent and her walk back towards the house, Temperance shook her head hard, for no other reason than to clear that gentleman out of her mind. By the time she had arrived home, however, she had still not succeeded.

Chapter Four

"Good evening, mother."

James smiled as his mother sat down at the table opposite him, ready to begin their dinner.

"Good evening," she smiled, looking a good deal happier than he had seen her in some months. "What a pleasant day this has been, has it not?"

James nodded. "I would quite agree." He gestured for the footmen to serve the first course. "I took a walk along the shore today and had a very pleasant time there."

His mother's eyebrows lifted. "It was rather windy, was it not?" she asked, as James nodded. "The summer is not yet upon us and here, being close to the sea, it can still sometimes feel as though we are in the depths of winter! Did you find yourself very cold?"

James shook his head. "No, not in the least. I found it rather refreshing, truth be told."

His mother smiled. "I am glad to hear it. I, for myself, took a short walk through the rose garden – though it is devoid of roses at the present moment – and thereafter, I did a little painting."

That made James smile. "You have not painted in some months."

"Ah but that is because I have not felt the urge to do so," came the quick reply, as his mother lifted the spoon of soup to her lips. "Today, however, I did."

"That is wonderful to hear. It has been a long time since you have done such a thing." James tilted his head. "Tell me, do you require anything in particular as regards your art? There is a shop in the village which, from what I recall, we can ask to send for whatever you need."

With a shake of her head, Lady Calverton smiled. "No, not at all. In fact, earlier today, I went to look for whatever I might have stored here and found a great abundance of things! I think I shall have plenty to hand."

James smiled and took a mouthful of soup, his mind returning to Lady Temperance, who he had met on the shore. "Speaking of art, mother, I found out that Lord and Lady Hartford still reside nearby and though Lord Hartford is absent from the house at the present moment, Lady Hartford is still present."

At this, his mother stared back at him for a long moment, only for her spoon to drop back down into her bowl.

"Mother?" James questioned, a little surprised at the expression which now crossed her face. "Are you quite well?"

Lady Calverton nodded, though her eyes immediately began to sparkle with hope. "Lady Hartford is present here? She is at home? I had thought that she might have gone to London for I do know just how much she loves society."

James shook his head. "It seems that her niece is staying with her and they are residing here at present. Lady Temperance did not make any mention of going to London."

At this remark, the light began to fade from his mother's expression. "Did you say Lady Temperance?"

James nodded. "Yes, I did. Why? Are you acquainted with her?" A knot tied itself in his stomach. "Is there something the matter? Ought I not to have associated with her?"

"You spoke with her? When?"

Realizing that he had not given any sort of explanation as to how he knew such things, James began his explanation. "I caught the lady as she stumbled down onto the shore. She had not come down by the path but had scrambled down a very dangerous way in order to catch a sketch which the wind had taken from her. I introduced myself and in that, found out that she was the niece of Lady Hartford and, in that, that the lady herself was still residing at the estate – and looks to be for the year, I should say given that Lady Temperance did not mention going to society or any such thing."

"Well, of course she would not go to society," came the reply. "Though I am glad to know that Lady Hartford is at home. I should *very* much like to call on her." A note of excitement came into her voice, sending a broad smile across her face. "I shall write a note to her this very evening!"

James smiled to himself, wondering silently what it would be like to be in company with Lady Temperance again. She had seemed rather shy when they had spoken on the shore but he could not blame her for that. The way she had kept her head turned away from him spoke of an uncertainty over their conversation, though that was more than a little understandable.

For a young lady to be speaking to a gentleman she did not know *and* without the presence of a chaperone was somewhat improper, though given their far-flung location and the lack of society present, James did not think that ought to be any concern. It was not as though a society gossip would come along and catch them in such a situation! His smile lingered as he considered the flash of gold in her curls as they had bounced around her temples, the emerald green of her eyes as she had darted a curious glance at him here and there.

"I wonder if Lady Hartford will be present at dinner tomorrow," his mother mused aloud, making James glance at her again, being pulled from his thoughts.

"Dinner tomorrow?"

His mother nodded. "Yes, I quite forgot to tell you that we received an invitation today from Lord and Lady Thurston. You did write to them to say that we would be arriving, yes?"

James nodded, his heart lifting as he thought of his dear friend, Lord Benjamin Thurston. They had played here together as boys, with Viscount Thurston's estate bordering his, and had even gone to Eton together. Lord Thurston had married a Lady Penelope some three years ago – around the very same time that James' brother had passed away. "Yes, I wrote to Thurston to inform him of our plans to spend a few months here."

"He is clearly looking forward to being in your company again!" His mother smiled. "And I am sure that you will be the very same. Though, as I have said, I wonder if Lady Hartford and her niece will be invited also? It was to a formal dinner and given that they are the only other society people present nearby, it should be expected that they would be present... though mayhap Lady Temperance is not at all eager to join even the smallest social events. I would not blame her, the poor child."

James blinked, then drew his eyebrows into a frown. "You speak as though there is something the matter? The young lady I spoke with appeared to be very contented indeed."

His mother's eyebrows lifted. "You did not see her face, then?"

James' frown deepened. "Yes, of course I did."

"Then you thought nothing of her scar?"

A little confused, James gazed back at his mother. "I did not see a scar." Understanding washed over him. "Ah, but that will be why she turned her head away from me. I thought it was to do with propriety or shyness but it probably was because she was attempting to hide that from me." When his mother nodded, James' heart filled with a sudden sympathy for the young lady. "I would not think less of her because of that."

"Yes, but that is because you are a gentleman of great character," came the reply, making James smile. "Her betrothed, the Marquess of Barlington, ended the engagement when he saw that the scar from her accident would be permanent."

A heavy darkness wrapped around James' mind and he scowled, hard. "What a cad."

"Indeed."

"Might I ask what happened? Do you know what the accident was?"

His mother nodded. "A horse threw her, I believe. It shied at something and she was flung from its back into a stone wall which ran along the perimeter of where she was riding. Lord Barlington was with her, as well as a few other guests." Perhaps seeing his confused look, his mother explained a little more clearly. "She was present at Lord Barlington's house party. A party to celebrate their engagement, I believe. It must have been dreadful for her to, first of all, recover from her injuries but, thereafter, to be forced to recover from a broken heart!" She clicked her tongue and shook her head. "Little wonder that she came to reside here. The *ton* did nothing but speak of it for a long time, from what I understand. We would not have been as aware of it, given that we were in our mourning period, but from my society friends, I understand that this is what was on society's lips for many a month. Very few people have seen Lady Temperance since that time and now, I should not expect her to return to London. Could you imagine what she would have to face? What she would have to endure?"

Recalling how the young lady had made certain to look away from him as best she could, remembering the glances she had sent him and realizing now that they came from uncertainty and, mayhap, even fear, James' lips twisted. "I can imagine it would not be pleasant."

"Indeed not." Lady Calverton let out a slow exhale of breath. "I do hope that the young lady will come to dinner, should an invitation have been given. It would be very pleasant to meet her."

"I am sure it shall," James murmured, his own thoughts returning to the young lady. He now found himself just as eager as his mother to greet Lady Temperance, finding himself a little intrigued by the lady. He wanted to be able to look her full in the face, to have her see that he was not about to be pushed away from her simply because of whatever scars she bore. That was not the sort of gentleman he was, though he could easily understand why she might fear such a thing from him.

"Lord Barlington must have no character whatsoever," he muttered to himself, though his mother nodded firmly. "To do such a thing to a young lady is quite dreadful!"

"It must have cost her dearly. She has endured a great deal and now, she must endure even more. Though did you say that she was pursuing a sketch?" A flicker of interest ignited her eyes and James smiled.

"Yes, that is what I said. It seems as though she is something of an artist, though I have not seen her work."

"That is something that we can talk about together, then!" Lady Calverton beamed at him from across the table. "I am all the more hopeful that she will be at dinner tomorrow, though if she is not, I am sure that I will make her acquaintance when I call on Lady Hartford."

James nodded. "I should like to join you, on your visit, whenever it is arranged."

"But of course. I think that this young lady will require as many acquaintances as she can – acquaintances who do nothing but accept her just as she is, acquaintances who can be trusted to treat her without mockery or disdain."

"You need not be concerned on my account," James protested, only for his mother to laugh and wave her hand.

"Yes, of course. I meant to suggest that *you* would be one such acquaintance," his mother explained, quickly. "Now, do let us get on and finish our dinner. I should like to write that note to Lady Hartford just as quickly as I can."

With a smile, James continued on with his meal, his thoughts still lingering on Lady Temperance. Silently wondering when he would get to see her again, he found himself smiling as he remembered the vivid green of her eyes and the golden hues of her hair. Scarred or not, Lady Temperance had certainly made an impression upon him, and it seemed that she was not someone he was likely to forget.

Chapter Five

"Are you quite ready?"

Temperance ran both hands down her gown and, turning to her aunt, nodded just as a knot tied itself in her stomach.

"You need not look so afraid," Lady Hartford murmured, gently. "My dear girl, it is only Lord and Lady Thurston."

"*And* Lord Calverton and his mother," Temperance reminded her, her thoughts going back to when the note had arrived the previous day, inviting them to a very hastily put together dinner, which would include Lord Calverton and his mother, Lady Calverton. Lady Thurston had apologized for the lateness of the invitation, stating that she had thought the notes had been sent out earlier in the week but had seemingly left them sitting at her writing desk rather than sending them. Temperance had immediately shaken her head, refusing to go to dinner with two strangers, afraid of what they would think of her, but her aunt had quietly encouraged her to change her mind, to put her fears to rest and to consider the kindness of Lady Thurston.

"Penelope is your dear friend. She has been away for six weeks now and upon her return, is clearly eager to be in your company again," Lady Hartford reminded her, as she drew Temperance away from the looking glass and towards the door of her bedchamber. "Both she and her husband have been nothing but kind to us both and you know very well that they would not have invited anyone to dinner who they knew would treat you with unkindness. Besides which, as I told you yesterday, I am very well acquainted with Lady Calverton and know that her character is both gracious and considerate. Her son, though I do not recall being introduced to him recently, will be just the same, I am sure." Her forehead puckered. "From what I recall my husband saying, I believe that this Lord Calverton is the younger son. Some years ago, there was news that the elder son had died from some foolishness which he had involved himself in – and this on the heels of his own father passing away! There seems to have been great pain placed upon the shoulders of both Lady Calverton and the newly titled Lord Calverton. Perhaps they have returned to this estate in order to recover a little from that."

Temperance frowned, her heart softening just a little towards the gentleman and his mother. "That sounds like a very sorrowful situation," she admitted, quietly. "I did not know that he was the younger son. I am surprised, however, that he has not made his way to London. I presume he is not married, if he is present with his mother."

Her aunt shook her head. "No, I do not think that he will be. Now come, do put a smile on your face! It is a very pleasant thing to go to dinner for we shall be in the company of both friends and new acquaintances and that will be a very joyous thing indeed."

Temperance nodded and swallowed at the knot in her throat, silently hoping that all that her aunt had said would come true. Lord Calverton had not seen her scar, not fully, at least, and she did not dare to think as to what his reaction might be when he *did* see her. Would he be as kind as her aunt believed? Or would there be shock there, disgust curling his lip as he turned his head away from her?

"Into the carriage," Lady Hartford said, urging Temperance gently into the carriage as though she feared she might turn around and run back into the house. "I am sure we will both be made very welcome indeed."

***

"I am thrilled that you were able to join us!"

The moment that Temperance stepped into the drawing room, she could not help but smile. Lady Thurston rushed across the room towards her, her hands outstretched as she captured Temperance's hands in hers and pressed tightly, a broad smile spreading right across her face.

"It was foolish of me to forget my invitations," she continued, as Temperance squeezed her hands back in return. "What a joy it is to me that you have been able to join us regardless!"

"It is good to see you," Temperance answered, smiling across the room to where Lord Thurston had also risen to greet them. "I did miss you last month. Did you enjoy your time in London?"

Lady Thurston immediately scowled. "No, I did not. The Season is not what it once was and I was relieved when it was time for us to return home. There are far too many gossips and far too much nonsense going on for us to enjoy even a moment there! When I was a debutante, there was still gossip, yes, but there was certainly not the same eagerness for scandal! I felt as though I was always being watched, that everything I did was being scrutinized. What a relief it was when Thurston's business was concluded and we could return home!" She smiled again and gestured to Temperance to sit down. "Tell me, have you been painting recently? I should very much like to see some of your more recent works. I am sure they are all quite wonderful."

"They are," Lady Hartford stated, before Temperance could say a word. "I believe that every time Temperance paints, her work improves. The last time I looked at her painting, it felt as though the sea itself was crashing right next to my feet, the salt stinging my cheeks."

Temperance blushed and quickly sat down, not wanting her aunt to speak with such fervor when it was not required. "My dear aunt is always very kind."

"And very honest too, I might add!" Lady Thurston added, making both Temperance and Lady Hartford smile. "You are much too inclined towards setting your work aside, refusing to consider it any good. You are always determined to make your next piece of work better, to improve yourself even more."

"Though that is what I think makes you so wonderful," her aunt interrupted again, as Lady Thurston nodded fervently. "And no, you need not look at me like that. I shall always think well of your work, my dear girl, no matter how much you should like to ignore that!"

Temperance laughed and was about to say how grateful she was for her aunt's remarks, only for the door to open and a gentleman and lady to step into the room, quickly followed by the butler.

"The Earl of Calverton and the Countess of Calverton," he announced – and Temperance's stomach dropped. She got to her feet and quickly dropped into a curtsy as Lady Thurston made the introductions, suddenly terribly afraid of what the gentleman and lady would think of her. The scar of her face felt hot, as though it had been seared with pain all over again, and Temperance's heart began to beat furiously. When she had been preparing for this evening's ball, Temperance had considered having the maid drape a few curls over one side of her face, hiding her scar a little, but then had decided not to do such a thing. She had no need to hide her face from Penelope for they were friends and had been for some time, and there would be no purpose in hiding it from Lord Calverton and his mother. No doubt they would either know of what had happened to her or would hear of it very soon once they saw her, and attempting to pretend she did not bear such a scar would be foolish indeed. It was much too obvious, much too prominent and to pretend she was something she was not was not worth either the time or the effort it would take to prepare her.

Courage, Temperance, her heart whispered to her as she lifted her chin and looked directly back at Lady Calverton. *There is nothing for you to fear.*

"How very glad I am to make your acquaintance, Lady Temperance!" With a voice filled with warmth and evident delight, Lady Calverton hurried towards her and, just as Lady Thurston had done, grasped her hand and pressed it gently. "Your aunt and I were very dear friends for some time, many years ago, and it is my joy to be not only in her company again, but also in yours." With a smile, she released Temperance's hand and then turned to Lady Calverton. They greeted each other with warm effusions and Temperance could not help but smile – only for her attention to be caught by the steady gaze of Lord Calverton.

A prickling climbed up her back as she looked back into his face, only for his eyes to dart away. Heat began to spiral up her chest as hot tears sprang up behind her eyes. Evidently, Lord Calverton was *not* of the same ilk as his mother. Was he shocked by her appearance? Horrified, even? Perhaps she ought not to have hidden herself from him when they had first met for then he would have known what to expect upon seeing her. She watched as he made his way towards Lord Thurston who not only greeted him warmly but began to talk at length, with neither gentleman giving her so much as a glance. Temperance herself turned towards her aunt and Lady Thurston, going to join their conversation, only for Lady Calverton to turn back towards her.

"Lady Temperance, I do hope that my son has not done anything wrong in telling me this, but he stated that he met you on the beach as you pursued a sketch?"

Evidently hearing this, Lord Calverton harrumphed and quickly walked across the room towards them all, making Temperance's heart quicken.

"My dear Lady Temperance," he said, bowing towards her. "Do excuse my mother. I did beg her not to speak to you of such a thing until you had brought the subject to hand but it appears that she will not listen!"

Temperance blinked, a little surprised at the gentleman's candor but also at the way he shook his head to his mother, who waved a hand and laughed, evidently not taking the least bit of consideration to what had been said.

"I thought to remain across the room to give you ladies an opportunity to talk," he said, explaining without realizing it, why he had stayed back from Temperance, "but now it seems I must come and encourage my mother to stop asking you such things as that! Mother, please." With a sigh, he turned to look at his mother, a slight sternness about his serious expression though Lady Calverton only laughed and shook her head.

"My son is a little too protective, I am sure," she said, though the smile she offered Temperance came with a slightly searching gaze. "I am someone who is very fond indeed of drawing, painting and the like. It brings me a great deal of joy to speak of it with someone who understands such a passion. Do you feel the same way, Lady Temperance?"

A little overwhelmed – both with Lord Calverton's obvious protectiveness expressed towards her and the questions that his mother had sent towards her – Temperance tried to smile and spread out both hands. "I am afraid that I do not often speak of my art, Lady Calverton."

"Though I think she is excellent in all that she does," chimed in her aunt, as Temperance sent a sharp look towards her, praying that she would not begin to praise her work all over again. "Temperance, however, does prefer to paint in solitude and I loathe to interrupt her."

"I quite understand," Lady Calverton said, directing a smile back towards Temperance. "What is it that you find you are drawn to? Is it the sea? The cliffs? The moorland? There are so many wonderful scenes here which cry out to be captured, are there not?"

"Please, Lady Temperance, do not feel as though you must answer every question here," Lord Calverton interrupted, putting his hand on his mother's arm. "Mother, please. You are very passionate about your drawing, I know, but you must not press the lady."

Temperance managed to smile as she looked into Lord Calverton's eyes, a little surprised at the softness about his hazel eyes which settled against the firm pull of his lips. Much to her surprise, he did not once look at her cheek, did not let his gaze pull towards her scar. Whether that was deliberate or not, she did not know but all the same, she greatly appreciated it.

"I apologise," Lady Calverton sighed, though the twinkle in her eyes lingered. "Lady Temperance, whenever you might wish to speak of your artistic work, please be aware that I should be very glad indeed to listen to all you have to say. I should very much like to share my passion so mayhap, you might be willing to call upon me one day also!"

Lord Calverton cleared his throat and his mother shot him a quick look before rolling her eyes and making Temperance smile.

"That is the dinner gong." With a warm smile, Lady Thurston directed them towards the door which would lead out to the dining room. "Shall we make our way there? I am certain that this conversation can continue over some excellent food and wine!"

Lady Calverton agreed enthusiastically and stepped away, just as Lady Hartford and Lord Thurston walked away together.

She was left looking to Lord Calverton, who, much to her astonishment, smiled, turned and offered her his arm.

"I must apologise for my mother," he said as she, somewhat tentatively, put her hand to his arm. "She is much too enthusiastic though it *has* been some time since she was able to speak about such things with anyone." He offered her a small smile as they followed after the others. "To be truthful, she has not even looked at a pencil or a paintbrush for some years. Now, however, we have returned here and within a sennight, she is talking about beginning to paint again! There must be something about this place that brings such an enthusiasm back to her."

"I can understand that," Temperance found herself saying, still a little overcome by all that had happened. "I find this place to be quite marvelous and in that regard, I cannot help but want to capture it as often as I can." She glanced up at him again, seeing him nod slowly as though he were trying to understand but could not quite do so. This was not the fellow she had thought him to be when he had first stepped into the room. She had been certain that the way he had looked at her and then stepped towards Lord Thurston had been because of her scar whereas now, she realized that he had only done such a thing in order to give opportunity for his mother to speak with the other ladies in the room. She had been quick to presume, quick to judge and he had proven her wrong in all that she had thought.

"I am afraid that I do not paint or even sketch!" he told her, as they entered the dining room. "I have no skill whatsoever in that regard, though I certainly do *appreciate* art. I have many a painting in my manor house and at the estate." Leading her to her chair, he released her hand and then pulled the chair out for her. "If you ever have opportunity to present your work, I certainly would be glad to see it. I am sure it is quite wonderful."

"Thank you, Lord Calverton." Temperance's heart leapt as he smiled, the action pulling away the seriousness from his hazel eyes. "I will consider it, of course. As I have said, it has been some time since I have shown anyone my work."

"Then I shall be all the more honoured if I ever have opportunity to see it," he smiled, before making his way to his own chair which was opposite her at the table. Temperance followed him with her eyes before dropping her gaze to her lap. This dinner had already gone a good deal better than she had expected and that brought such relief to her, she could barely speak. With a smile and a set of her shoulders, Temperance looked around the room and caught her aunt looking at her. Temperance's smile grew as her aunt gave her a small nod, clearly aware that all of Temperance's fears had been chased away. The first course was served and Temperance joined in with the others in conversation, though now and again, her gaze snagged on Lord Calverton. Never once did he look anywhere other than her eyes, never once did he glance at her marred cheek. For the first time in many a month, Temperance felt herself relax entirely at this social occasion. Perhaps she *would* show her artwork to Lady Calverton. Perhaps she would be bold enough to share some of her paintings with others rather than keep hiding them away and, only on occasion, sharing them with her aunt. There was a fresh encouragement in

Lady Calverton's enthusiasm and Temperance found herself smiling at the thought.

This year might turn out to be a little better than she had ever permitted herself to hope. She might have new acquaintances, new friendships and, mayhap, a new lease of life with it.

Chapter Six

"Mother?"

Walking into the drawing room, James stopped sharply, his breath catching in his chest as he took in the scene before him. Lady Calverton was standing before an easel, paintbrush in hand with a tray of paint on the table to her right. There were papers everywhere, lying at her feet and on the chair to her left and he dared not let his eyes go to the paint tray for fear that he would see paint dripping on the carpet between that and the easel.

"Ah, there you are! I did wonder when you would return from your ride." Lady Calverton turned towards him, the brightness in her eyes making James smile despite the scene. There was a smudge of paint on her cheek, a flush of color in her face and James found himself rather relieved that she was wearing an apron over her gown.

"Good afternoon, mother," he said, coming a little more cautiously into the room. "Goodness, might I ask what has brought this about?"

"Oh, it was in speaking with Lady Temperance!" came the reply. "She did not say much about her art, granted, but there was such a passion in what she *did* say that I could not help but take out everything I have and begin to paint!"

James frowned. "I did not think that she said anything."

"She did not say anything to *you*, mayhap. But when you stayed with Lord Thurston to take a glass of port, we ladies retired to the drawing room for tea and there, we were able to speak about a good many things."

James closed his eyes. "Mama, I do hope you did not press her on such things. It seemed to me as though she was a little reluctant."

"She is simply not used to it, that is all," his mother stated, waving a hand – a hand which held the paintbrush and James eyed it nervously, worried that a splash of paint might fling itself onto his shirt. "I am going to call on Lady Hartford tomorrow afternoon and I hope that Lady Temperance will be present also and would be willing to show me even one of her sketches."

Silently wondering if he ought to write in advance of his mother's visit to apologise for her fervency, James bit his lip to keep those words from escaping.

"I am sure that, after a little more encouragement, Lady Temperance and I will be able to share our artistic passions," his mother sighed, seemingly quite contented with all that she hoped for. "Goodness, it is quite marvelous how this has all returned to me so quickly! It has been a long time since I felt the desire to draw. In fact, I believe the last time I did so was before your father passed away."

At the mention of this, James' stomach twisted. "That has been a very long time indeed then, mother. Years, in fact."

"Something he would not have liked," she replied, smiling softly. "I know that you would have preferred that I found another place to paint but the view from the window was simply begging me to paint it and – "

"If you are happy, mother, then please, do not concern yourself with where you are painting," James interrupted, gently putting one hand on his mother's shoulder and seeing her smile. "I am glad to see you doing so again."

She smiled at him. "You are very generous, Calverton. I do hope that when I speak with Lady Temperance, I will have some recent work to speak of...so I must continue painting and finish this piece given that we are to call on her soon."

"I am certain you shall finish it very soon," James remarked, turning on his heel and making to quit the room. "I shall leave you in solitude so you might continue on without interruption."

His mother smiled and waved her paintbrush at him in farewell before James closed the door tightly, silently praying that his drawing room would not be too paint-splattered by the time evening came.

Humming to himself, James made his way back along the hall to where his study was situated, genuinely considering writing a letter to Lady Temperance, apologizing for his mother's fervor and warning her of the fervor still to come! Pausing for a moment, he glanced out of the window towards the shoreline, finding his heart filling with a sense of happiness as he took in the way the sunlight beamed down from the sky through what was otherwise thick, grey clouds. There was a simple joy in watching that, in seeing the light shine down as it did.

I wonder if Lady Temperance is outside also, sketching the scene as she did when I first met her.

A flickering interest grew as he turned away from his study and instead, made for the door. With a word to his butler that he was going to take a short stroll, James hurried outside and made his way along the familiar path, finding his hopes growing with every step. Mayhap he would not have to write a note to Lady Temperance after all. Mayhap he would be able to speak to her face to face.

The wind blew a good deal more gently than it had done over the last few days and the sun, when it broke through the clouds, was warm on his cheek. Making his way to the top of the cliffs, James looked to the left and to the right, only to spy a figure down on the shore. A broad smile spread across his face as he turned to hurry along to the path, hoping that Lady Temperance had made her way down to the shore using the path rather than scrambling down as she had done before! Keeping that smile fixed, he made his way towards her, noticing how her head lifted and then dropped again as she sketched furiously on a piece of paper. Suddenly not wanting to interrupt her, James paused for a moment, his hands going behind his back as he watched her. The left side of her face was visible to him and, since he had never let himself do so before, James let his gaze trace the scar there. It ran a red line down from just below her eyes, fading a little at the bottom but rather than feeling any sort of dislike or dismay, James felt nothing but sadness for all that she had endured. The injury would have been one thing but to have one's betrothed step back from you was quite another!

He smiled to himself as Lady Temperance's hand continued to sketch wildly across the paper, her head continuing to bob up and down as she took in the scene. The clouds began to move a little more speedily now, the wind blowing heavier gusts across the sky, and James watched as Lady Temperance's shoulders dropped. Her hand fell to her side, the other still holding her sketch as the scene before them changed entirely.

With a sigh, she turned, only to let out a shriek, stumbling back in shock.

"Forgive me!" James exclaimed, coming closer to her as Lady Temperance heaved in a great breath, her hand at her heart, her pencil nowhere to be seen. "I did not want to interrupt you."

Lady Temperance shook her head, still gasping for breath as she stared at him, wide-eyed.

"Your sketch, Lady Temperance!" Seeing the wind attempting to tug it out of her fingers, James hurried forward, helping her to fold it back carefully into her book though, as his eyes took in her work, his heart flooded with admiration at her skill. His hand touched hers for a brief moment and a sudden burst of fire ran up through his veins, leaving him to breathe a little more quickly as he stepped back from her again.

"You gave me such a fright, Lord Calverton." Lady Temperance looked away from him, her lips flattening for a moment. "I think I have dropped my pencil also."

Spying it, James reached for it, taking it out of the sand and handing it back to her. "Forgive me," he said, again. "I did not mean to startle you. I had hoped that you would be here, however. I did want to speak with you, to apologise for last evening."

Her eyebrows lifted, golden curls still bouncing gently at her temples, her bonnet ribbons blowing across her shoulders.

"I want to apologise for my mother's fervency in her questions and in her constant chatter as regards your artistic abilities," he continued, not wanting her to be confused as to his question. "I know that she was rather intensive in her questioning and I was rather concerned that you were somewhat uncomfortable. I know that you are to be subject to my mother's visit again tomorrow and I have, I assure you, asked her not to do the very same thing as she was doing last evening! I do not know if she will do as I have asked, however, so I thought it best to not only apologise to you but also apologise in advance for what she may do."

Much to his surprise, Lady Temperance not only smiled but let out a laugh which made James' eyebrows lift in astonishment. The smile spread a glorious light all through her expression, making his own lips curve upwards also.

"You came to warn me about your mother?" she asked, as James found himself chuckling, though he nodded as he did so. "Goodness, Lord Calverton, she was not as bad as you think. I thought her enthusiasm rather kind, and in truth, I am glad to know that there is someone else who paints and draws as I do."

"But you did not seem eager to answer her many questions," James protested, though his smile remained. "I do not want you to think that you must answer every one she throws at you."

Lady Temperance's smile softened and she lifted her shoulders gently before letting them fall again. "I am rather shy about speaking about my work, yes," she admitted, her gaze darting away from him again, "but I am not particularly used to company and certainly not to *new* company either! It takes a great deal of strength for me to speak of such things though my aunt assures me that your mother is genuine in her desire to know of my work."

A little confused, James nodded. "Of course she is genuine. Why would she not be so?"

Her smile turned a little sorrowful and she looked away from him, gazing out to the sea. "Some might speak of it out of pity," she said, a little more quietly. "They might wish to express an interest out of sympathy towards me which, of course, is very kind but still lacks sincere interest."

James put one hand out to her for a moment, then dropped it back to his side. "I can assure you, my mother is nothing but sincere. When I left her, she was busy painting in the drawing room, eager to have something to discuss with you when she comes to call tomorrow afternoon."

A flicker of interest grew in Lady Temperance's eyes. "Is that so?" Her lip curled gently. "Is your drawing room going to be quite all right? My aunt has given me a place to paint by the window that looks out to the sea but there is a great many covers and the like on everything, for fear that I will splash paint on it!"

James laughed and put one hand to his forehead for a moment. "Alas, my mother has not been so considerate, Lady Temperance. I shall return home at this very moment and have my staff do that at once, in the hope that no further damage will occur!"

She laughed again and James smiled warmly, glad that he had seen a smile upon the lady's face. How different this conversation had been from the first time they had met on the shore!

"Are you to linger here a little longer? Or are you going to walk back to the path?"

Lady Temperance looked out to the sea for a moment before she answered. "I think I shall linger here for a little longer. The scene has changed, yes, but I may still sketch a little longer."

"Very well." James inclined his head. "Good afternoon, Lady Temperance."

"Wait a moment."

He turned back to her. "Yes?"

"Are... are you to join your mother in your visit tomorrow?"

James hesitated, not certain as to whether she was asking because she desired such a thing or because she was less eager for his company. "I am not yet certain."

She smiled again though this time, it was not as wide as it had been before. "You are most welcome, of course. I should not like you to think that you would not be welcome to join your mother."

James smiled, thanked her and then turned to make his way back to the path. As he walked, he glanced back to see her standing on the shore, looking out to the waves but doing nothing else.

His heart twisted with uncertainty. Was it that she wanted him to join his mother in her visit tomorrow? Or was she simply being polite with such an invitation? James did not know and as he continued his walk back along the path, he found himself more and more confused. What would be best? What was it that Lady Temperance wanted? And what was it that he himself desired?

Chapter Seven

"You *will* speak to Lady Calverton this afternoon, will you not?"

"Of course I will speak to her," Temperance answered, a little confused as to her aunt's question. "Why would I not?"

Her aunt shook her head. "That is not what I meant. I did not mean to suggest that you would not speak to her about all manner of things, only whether you would speak to her of your artwork."

Temperance frowned. "I do not have any intention of showing her any of my work, though I am happy to speak of it."

"But why would you not *show* it?"

Reluctance curled in Temperance's stomach. "Aunt, my work is very private. It is personal to me. It means a great deal to me and I am not particularly inclined towards revealing it to those I am not well acquainted with yet."

"I can understand that but – "

"Besides which, I spoke to Lord Calverton yesterday afternoon and he told me that I was not to feel any sort of pressure to answer her questions. I am more than happy to discuss art and the like, but whether or not I will show her any of my work is quite another matter."

"I understand." Taking in a deep breath, her aunt set her hands on her knees and then leaned forward in her chair. "I must also inform you that your mother and father wish to come to visit."

Temperance blinked in surprise. "To visit? I thought they would have gone to London."

"I presume there is very little point in their going there," came the reply. "Your sisters are wed and settled and aside from collecting society gossip and, mayhap, playing a few games of cards, there is no purpose for your parents to make their way there. Therefore, I have been informed that they wish to come to reside here for a short time. We are to expect them within a sennight."

Temperance's heart slammed hard against her chest. "It has already been decided?"

"Well, it is not as though I could refuse!" Her aunt smiled gently. "Have no fear, my dear niece. There is nothing about their presence that should frighten you."

"Aside from the fact that the last letter my mother sent was to encourage me back to London society," Temperance breathed, softly. "What if her purpose in coming here is to force me back there?"

"Then you can be assured that I will not permit her to do so," Lady Hartford stated, firmly. "I am with you in this. I understand your reluctance to return to society, having every awareness of what you will face. I will not permit her to reign in this. Your mother is many things, my dear, and has many good qualities but her desire to have all of her daughters wed and settled is her sole, prevailing desire and does not come from any genuine consideration of your circumstances. Trust me when I say that I will do all I can to protect you from that."

Temperance nodded, her concern growing all the more. "My father might – "

"Your father has never suggested that you return to society," her aunt interjected. "I do not know if he feels as strongly as your mother. It may be that he is simply looking for a little respite away from his responsibilities, just as Lord Calverton is doing."

"I must hope so," Temperance murmured, her concerns tightening like a noose around her neck. "You say that they are arriving next week?"

"Yes. But there is enough company here to keep your mother distracted!" Her aunt laughed, just as the door opened. "And speaking of company... "

"Lord Calverton and Lady Calverton, my lady." The butler bowed as their two guests walked into the room, just as Temperance and her aunt rose to their feet, ready to greet them. Temperance's stomach twisted with a sudden sharpness as she realized that Lord Calverton *had* chosen to come along with his mother, rather than remain at home. She had not been certain whether or not he had intended to join her but had wanted to make clear to him that he was more than welcome. It had not been because of any personal considerations, of course, but simply so that he knew she was not hiding herself away. He was a gentleman that, thus far, appeared to be trustworthy and considerate, for he had not looked at her scar and had not mocked her for it either.

The way he had come to find her, to seek her out so that he might apologise for his mother's eagerness, had made her all the more confident of his character and she was glad that he had chosen to come.

"Good afternoon!" Lady Hartford exclaimed, welcoming them both into the room. "Jenkins, the tea tray, if you please."

The butler nodded and excused himself, leaving Temperance to take her seat again as Lady Calverton sat next to Lady Hartford and Lord Calverton sat opposite. The atmosphere in the room was warm rather than tense and Temperance immediately found herself at ease.

"My son decided to accompany me for fear that I would quite terrify Lady Temperance with my many questions as regards her artwork," Lady Calverton began, shooting a look towards her son which made not only him but both Temperance and her aunt smile. "I believe that is being a little over-protective but mayhap I *am* being a little *too* strong with my questions!" Her eyes went to Temperance who smiled quickly. "It is only that I have not had anyone to speak with about such things – it is very difficult to find someone who truly understands."

"I know what you mean," Temperance agreed, as Lady Calverton beamed back at her. "I am quite happy to answer any questions, Lady Calverton."

"Though my mother has promised that she will not ask too many," Lord Calverton interjected, his tone a little dark and his expression serious though his mother only smiled. "And she will not press you either, Lady Temperance."

Temperance chuckled softly. "I thank you, I am certain we will be able to speak without too much difficulty."

"Though my niece does not want to show any of her work as yet," Lady Hartford added, making Temperance's smile fade. "I am sure that you, as a fellow artist, can understand, Lady Calverton!"

"Oh, of course!" Lady Calverton exclaimed, before turning to Temperance and beginning to speak about the process of her art and asking Temperance a good many questions about what she herself experienced and went through as regarded choosing what to draw or paint. Temperance answered as best as she could, aware of the way Lord Calverton's gaze went from both herself and then to his mother and back again. The conversation flowed easily enough, with both Lady Calverton and Lady Hartford asking

Temperance various questions, which surprised Temperance a little. Surely her aunt knew a little more about her art than this? But then, Temperance considered, she had never really spoken to her aunt about her need to paint, about the prevailing force which pushed her to paint, which pushed her to stand at the window, gaze out at the scene before her and paint it with fresh abandon. Her aunt gave her a space to paint, gave her all that she needed but had never really asked Temperance about it. No doubt that had been out of consideration for her, giving her the time and the space she required and, in thinking on that, Temperance was suddenly overwhelmed with a great affection for her aunt. How kind Lady Hartford had been to her in all of this! She had not only given her a place to live, but had welcomed her there with love, kindness and consideration. It was more than her mother had shown her, certainly, and for that, Temperance was more than grateful.

"Ah, and now the tea tray has arrived!" Lady Hartford exclaimed, giving Temperance a smile. "Might you pour the tea, Temperance?"

"It would be my pleasure." Finding herself truly delighted not only with the company she was in but also with how easy the conversation had been, Temperance smiled and rose to her feet.

"Tell me, Lord Calverton, how long do you expect to be here?" Lady Hartford asked, as Temperance set out each cup and saucer in front of each person present. "Are you to be here for some months?"

Lord Calverton nodded. "Yes, I think so. I have no desire to return to London for the Season, I confess. My mother graciously agreed to come back to this estate for a short while. It has been some time since I have been able to take a rest from my responsibilities – and many years since I have been present here!"

"Did you come here as children?" Temperance asked, as Lord Calverton nodded.

"Yes. My brother and I – may he rest in peace – used to have many a fond holiday here. We would climb the cliffs, chase the rabbits across the moorland and, on occasion, swim in the sea."

"Much to his mother's chagrin!" Lady Calverton exclaimed, making Temperance laugh as she resumed her seat. "This is to be my dower house, you see, Lady Temperance. Once my son decides to marry, I shall settle here and I shall be very contented, I am sure."

"It would be a pleasure to have you as a neighbour again," Lady Hartford smiled. "Lord Calverton, I think that you should do as your mother clearly desires and find a young lady to wed! That way, she can retire to the dower house and all will be well."

For whatever reason, Temperance found herself flushing hot, glancing to Lord Calverton and hearing the few seconds of silence which followed her aunt's statement. Surely neither her aunt nor Lady Calverton thought that there might be a match made here between Lord Calverton and herself!

"I shall seek to take your advice as soon as I am able, Lady Hartford," Lord Calverton said after a few more moments, though there was a note of laughter in his voice as though he knew that there was nothing but jesting here. "Though I confess that I will not be making my way to London any time soon. Society does not interest me, as I am sure you can understand. My brother's untimely death would be the source of much conversation should I return there. Gossip is something greatly distressing and I have no desire to be a part of it."

Temperance nodded, her expression pulling flat. "It is much too inclined towards gossip and the like," she agreed, softly, understanding exactly what it was he meant. "Why should anyone want to be a part of a society which values such a thing? Something which causes pain and sorrow to those who are spoken about?"

Lord Calverton shared a look with her which spoke of pain and Temperance's heart plunged low. She did not know what it was that Lord Calverton had meant as regarded his brother, did not understand what had caused his death, but neither did she *need* to know. That was the trouble with the *ton*. They needed to know everything that was taking place, felt it something which *had* to be shared and, thereafter, talked about but all that did was leave pain behind in its place.

"You are not about to make your way to London, then?" Lady Calverton asked gently, as Temperance shook her head. "Then I look forward to having very engaging company for the next few months! We shall have dinners and soirees and mayhap even a ride here and there?"

A shudder ran through Temperance and she closed her eyes briefly though her aunt quickly responded to Lady Calverton, taking away the requirement for Temperance to answer. All at once, the memory of riding across the gardens with Lord Barlington came back to her, flooding her entire being with a chill which shook her frame. Opening her eyes, she reached to take a sip of her tea, aware of the slight tremble in her hand as she did so. The warmth of the liquid chased away a little of the cold from her frame as she set it back down again.

"Excuse me for a moment, if you please." Temperance forced a smile as she rose to her feet and then stepped away, walking out of the drawing room and into the hallway. Her feet took her to the parlor, her place of solitude, the place where she painted, and opening the door, Temperance stepped inside, closed the door and leaned back against it for a moment.

I did not think this would trouble me so greatly still.

Opening her eyes, Temperance made her way across the room and stood by the easel. The painting she had done the most recently – albeit not finished – comforted her for a moment, reminding her of the moment she had stood on the shore and sketched the way the beams of light from the sun which had spread down towards the sea. Temperance closed her eyes, grounding herself in that moment, waiting for peace to wash over her.

A quiet rap at the door made Temperance's eyes fly open and as she turned, she saw none other than Lord Calverton standing there. One hand remained on the door handle, clearly unwilling to step in after her – mayhap for the sake of propriety, she did not know.

"I wanted to make certain you were all right, Lady Temperance." Coming a little further into the room, he spread out both hands, the door still wide open. "I do not think that my mother thought for a moment that making such a suggestion would upset you. She spoke without thinking."

Temperance's heart softened as she tried to smile. "Of course she did not. I do not think that it was deliberate on her part, not at all."

Lord Calverton nodded. "And you are quite all right?" The way his hazel eyes searched hers made Temperance smile, her hands going to her heart.

"Yes, I am. I will take a few moments and then return to you all."

"Very well." Lord Calverton continued to study her for a few moments and then with a nod, stepped away.

Temperance closed her eyes, took in a long breath and then let it out again slowly. Her heart squeezed but it was not with pain. It was with a sense of happiness, of warmth, that he had thought to come and see if she was all right. Evidently, he knew what had happened to her – mayhap his mother had informed him – and yet he had not turned away from her. He had, instead, shown more compassion and consideration that even her own sisters had done when the accident had first taken place.

"He is a good man," Temperance murmured to herself, opening her eyes again as she looked back at her canvas. "A very good man indeed."

Chapter Eight

James clicked to his horse, having permitted it to amble along the road for some minutes. They had enjoyed a good canter on their way back to the manor house but now, the horse was getting tired and, the truth was, so was he. He and his mother had taken a long walk around the small village, taking in everything and making certain to purchase something from each and every shop. There were only a few, yes, but he wanted to make certain that all of them received some of his custom. Thereafter, his mother had returned with the carriage but James had chosen to take a ride around the area, seeking out a little solitude. It had been a pleasant ride but he was now ready to return home.

The sound of hooves behind him made James turn, only to see the smiling face of Lord Thurston approaching.

"Thurston!" he exclaimed, as his friend drew his horse close beside him. "Good afternoon! I did not think that I would see you."

"No?"

James chuckled at his friend's enquiring look. "No, not when we are to have a soiree at your manor house this evening."

"Ah, but there is very little to do," came the reply. "Besides which, my dear lady wife does prefer to take on all the arrangements. I am not to say a single word to her about it, in fact, but I am to trust that all will be well and, to be truthful, every time I have done so, it had been just as she promised so I have every faith in her."

Smiling, James found himself considering what it would be like to be married. Would he have the very same confidence in his own bride, whoever that might prove to be? Would she desire to take on the running of the home and of all the occasions they might put on? For whatever reason, his thoughts suddenly turned to Lady Temperance and, as her face flashed before his eyes, James shook his head and harrumphed, chasing the image away.

His friend lifted an eyebrow enquiringly but James only shrugged, choosing not to explain his strange reaction.

"Did you hear that the Duke and Duchess of Danfield are to come to stay?" his friend asked, as James frowned. "I hear they are to arrive at the end of the week."

"The Duke of Danfield? I do not think I am acquainted with him or his wife."

Lord Thurston smiled briefly. "They are Lady Temperance's parents. Lady Temperance told Penelope only yesterday about the news, though she did not appear to be particularly pleased about seeing them."

"I wonder why that should be."

Lord Thurston opened his mouth to say something more, only to snap it closed again and to shake his head. "I will not go into prolonged explanations, only to say that I believe the Duchess is very keen for her daughter to return to society."

James' eyebrows lifted. "But society will only speak ill of her! They will mock and whisper about her behind her back and that will bring her only more pain!"

"Precisely. Thankfully, I think that Lady Hartford is very eager indeed to do as her niece wants and will defend her from such a thing. It is good that she is willing to support her niece in that way."

"Indeed it is," James answered, now thinking very highly of Lady Hartford. "I am surprised that the Duchess would encourage her daughter back into such a situation."

"It is, mayhap the only way that she can see for her daughter to marry and, from what I understand, that is the hope of every mother: for their daughter to marry well."

James bit his lip and refused to say anything more. He wanted to begin to ask why the Duchess of Danfield could not see the pain that being brought back to society would cause Lady Temperance but instead chose to remain quite silent. The chances of the young lady finding a suitable match were very slim indeed, even if she *were* to return to society. The gentlemen of the *ton* were very specific in their requirements for a wife and James could not think of a single one who would look past her scar.

Though I would.

The thought sent heat rippling down his spine as he turned his head away from Lord Thurston for fear that his friend would see the heat in James' cheeks.

"I do think that – oh, good gracious!"

James turned his head just as Lord Thurston pulled his horse to the side of the road. The rumble of carriage wheels signaled the arrival of a carriage which was coming much too quickly, giving

James only a few seconds to pull his horse to the same side as Lord Thurston. The carriage did not slow and James' horse immediately shied as it rushed up alongside them. With all of his strength and his skill, James kept it under control, though both he and Lord Thurston let out an angry roar to the driver and the occupants within the carriage as it rushed past them.

"Goodness, whatever fool was that?" James exclaimed, bringing his horse back towards the center of the road, alongside Lord Thurston. "Do they not know that this is a country road? That there are other occupants upon it?"

"Clearly, they do not," Lord Thurston answered, his voice holding a note of disgust. "Simpletons, certainly."

As though the carriage driver had heard them, the carriage began to slow and, as James and Lord Thurston continued to ride, came to a complete stop. Thereafter, the carriage door opened and a gentleman stepped out.

James frowned and threw a look to Lord Thurston. "If this gentleman attempts to say that we are at fault, I shall have a few choice words to say to him!" he exclaimed, though he kept his voice low. "Whatever was he thinking forcing the driver to rush ahead like that?"

"Gentlemen!" The fellow spread out both hands, his smile broad despite the fact that his driver had almost caused an accident. "I do hope you are both all right. I do not know what my driver was thinking!"

Choosing to remain astride his horse, James brought his mount to a stop only a few steps away from the gentleman. To his mind, this gentleman was already speaking untruths, for the driver would not have driven in such a way without having been instructed to by his master. "We are both quite all right," he said, a little snippily. "That was a most imprudent action, I must say. Compelling your coachman to urge your horses to hasten their pace on such treacherous roads does not bode well for our safety." He arched an eyebrow as the still smiling gentleman opened his mouth, only for him to snap it closed again. Then, he shrugged.

"I will admit to telling my driver to make his way with urgency. I am greatly desirous to be at the house."

Again, James and Lord Thurston shared a look.

"The house?" Lord Thurston asked, quickly. "I do not think we are introduced and I have resided here for many years. You are not one of our neighbours, I think."

The gentleman shook his head, beaming at Lord Thurston. "No, indeed not. However, I *am* to reside for a time in a small manor house which is nearby somewhere. It belongs to a friend of mine, Lord Grayson."

Lord Thurston's eyebrows lifted. "Lord Grayson has gone to London for the Season."

"Yes, and has granted me permission to reside in his manor house here," the gentleman explained. "It is still some miles away from what I understand."

Lord Thurston nodded. "Five miles from here," he said, making James' brows drop low as the gentleman's smile finally began to fade. "It will still take you some time to reach there. Might I ask why you have such an urgency? You will need to be careful with your horses. The road can be a little stony in places and they will need to be cautious... unless you want a lame horse."

The gentleman nodded, now looking rather solemn. "I quite understand. Thank you. I will tell the driver to be more careful." His smile returned. "As regards for the urgency, it is because I am very keen to become reacquainted with an old acquaintance who resides nearby. I am coming without their knowledge, so it shall be something of a surprise so I must beg of you not to tell anyone that you have seen me!"

James' brows dropped even lower. Who was this gentleman? What acquaintance did he have around here? There was something about the glint in the gentleman's eyes and the broad, confident smile which whispered of arrogance and James did not much like pride in someone's character.

"We do not know your name, so how can we say anything?" he asked, as the gentleman laughed. "Though mayhap we ought to be introduced?" He inclined his head. "The Earl of Calverton and my friend, Lord Thurston."

The gentleman bowed. "Well, so long as I have your promise of silence, I shall introduce myself." He looked first at Lord Thurston and then to James, who, after a moment, both gave him a small nod. With a smile, the gentleman bowed again. "The Marquess of Barlington, at your service. And now that introductions have been made, I must take my leave of you! I am sure we shall see each other again very soon at some soiree or some such thing, given that you are clearly well acquainted with everyone else in this desolate place! Good afternoon to you both!"

With a cheery wave, Lord Barlington climbed back into his carriage which, after a moment, began to rattle along the road though, much to James' relief, at a much slower pace. With a shake of his head, he looked to Lord Thurston, only to see his friend's eyes wide with shock.

"Thurston? What is it?"

Lord Thurston blinked. "Do you not know that name?"

James shook his head slowly, only for a sudden recollection to hit him, hard. "Oh, no."

"Yes. That was the gentleman who broke of his engagement to Lady Temperance, once he saw the injury that she had sustained from her fall."

James closed his eyes briefly, fighting the furious urge to ride after the carriage and, once it had stopped, demand to know whether the person who was not expecting to see Lord Barlington was, in fact, Lady Temperance herself.

"You think that she does not know of his arrival," Lord Thurston murmured, as James nodded. "Yes, I think I would agree with that." He looked at James, one eyebrow lifted. "We did say that we would keep his secret, that we would not tell anyone of his arrival."

James scoffed immediately, his concern for Lady Temperance pushing aside everything else. "I have every intention of making certain she is aware of it," he stated, as Lord Thurston nodded. "It may be that she is already aware and mayhap it is someone else that the gentleman spoke of but, to be certain of it I have every intention of telling her of his arrival."

"Be cautious when you do so," Lord Thurston warned. "It will come as a great shock. She and Penelope are very dear friends and I know the great injury that his rejection caused Lady Temperance."

James nodded, glancing to the path and wondering if he ought to go to speak with her now rather than wait for the soiree this evening. "You will excuse me, Thurston?"

His friend's eyes flickered. "You wish to talk to Lady Temperance now?"

"I do. I think it would be best to do so at this moment rather than at the soiree. She may be overwhelmed and the soiree would be ruined for her."

Lord Thurston smiled briefly. "That is a wise thought. I hope she will still come to the soiree but yes, I think it would be wisest to make her aware of his presence now. I will see you this evening."

"Thank you, old friend." Without another word, James clicked to his horse, pushing it into a canter again. The urgency which drove him sent fire into his veins and as he came upon the house, his heart began to beat furiously. What would she say to this news? Would she be overcome with shock or fright? Or would she quietly be glad of Lord Barlington's arrival, perhaps hoping that their broken engagement might recover again?

Chapter Nine

"Temperance? Might you be able to join me for a cup of tea?"

Tilting her head to study her current work, Temperance paused and then nodded. "Yes, Aunt. I will join you in a few moments."

"Excellent. I – I have had another note from your mother, sent the day before she and your father left their home to travel here."

Hearing the note of concern in her aunt's voice, Temperance turned her head to look back at her. "They have not changed their plans, have they?"

Her aunt shook her head. "No, though... well, it does not matter. I will talk to you about the letter over tea." She withdrew and Temperance's frown lingered as she turned back to her painting. She did not know why but her fingers had itched to paint a single, solitary figure on the shoreline – though it was not herself that she drew. It was a gentleman, broad shouldered with a fine hat upon his head... and Temperance knew all too well that she had been thinking of Lord Calverton as she had drawn it. Quite why she had drawn him standing on the shore, she did not know but without his presence there, the painting had felt incomplete.

Smiling a little ruefully to herself, Temperance turned and, setting her paintbrush down, made her way to the drawing room where her aunt would be waiting. It was just as well she did not show her work to anyone save her aunt, for what would Lady Calverton or even Lord Calverton himself say, should he see it? Would he recognize himself? And if he did, what would he think of her painting him into the scene? Flushing with embarrassment at the very thought, Temperance stepped into the parlor, only to come to a sudden stop.

The very same gentleman she had only just been thinking of was seated beside her aunt and, as Temperance came into the room, he rose to greet her, bowing at the waist.

"Lord Calverton." Temperance blinked and then came to sit down, her heart quickening. "I was not expecting you. My aunt did not say that you had come to take tea with us; I can only apologise for my tardiness."

"No, not at all. I came unexpectedly, in the hope that I might speak with you."

"With me?" Temperance repeated, just as the tea tray was brought in. "On any specific matter?" For a moment, she feared that he was to ask her about her paintings, might beg to see some of them and she would have no other choice but to bring him into the parlor where she painted, leaving him to see the figure standing on the shoreline.

"Yes. I was out riding this afternoon after a somewhat prolonged excursion around the village and the shops there, when I met Lord Thurston."

Temperance set out the tea cups in front of them all, then sat back down so she might take a sip of her own cup. "I see." She did not understand why he should want to tell her of such a thing but, with a smile, Temperance waited for him to continue.

Lord Calverton's serious gaze soon chased that smile away.

"A carriage came rattling around the corner and would have run both Lord Thurston and myself off the road, had we not pulled our horses into the side. I was almost in the hedge myself and thought very poorly of the driver and the occupant within the carriage, for they ought not to drive in such a way! The carriage soon stopped and the gentleman within stepped out, making to apologise."

Temperance shared a look with her aunt, though, to her surprise, her aunt looked just as severe in her expression as Lord Calverton did. Whatever was the matter?

"This gentleman *did* apologise and, after a few minutes of conversation, stated that he was to stay in Lord Grayson's manor house, since he has gone to London for the Season."

"Lord Grayson resides some four miles away from here," her aunt told Temperance as though that was somehow significant. "It is a short distance on horseback."

Temperance frowned, looking to her aunt and then to Lord Calverton. "Is there something about this gentleman that I ought to know?"

"I think there is, yes. I was going to speak with you this evening but I did not want the soiree to be ruined for you.

Therefore, despite my promise to the gentleman that I would not speak of his presence here, I think it best that I tell you his name."

"I do not want you to break your word to him, however," Temperance exclaimed, before he could say another word. "There is surely no need. It is imperative that a gentleman is known to be able to keep his word." A vision of Lord Barlington came back to her mind, for he was certainly *not* a gentleman who did as he had promised. For some reason, she felt that Lord Calverton would be betraying himself if he did such a thing, wanted him to be as good a gentleman as she believed him to be. "Why did he want you to keep his presence a secret?"

"Listen to Lord Calverton, my dear," her aunt interjected. "I am aware of what he has to tell you and it is for a good purpose."

Lord Calverton's jaw tightened. "This gentleman desired that his presence be kept from everyone because, as he told Lord Thurston and myself, it is to be a surprise for the person he is coming to see. That person, I believe, is you, Lady Temperance."

Shock rifled through her chest. "Me?"

The gentleman nodded. "Lord Barlington has come to reside here, Lady Temperance."

If Temperance had not been sitting down, she would have collapsed such was the weakness which ran through her. She could not take her eyes from Lord Calverton, her breathing ragged and her chest tight.

"The note I received from your mother confirms this," Lady Hartford said, softly. "That was why I wanted to speak with you. It seems that Lord Barlington came to beg forgiveness from both your father and your mother, with the sole intention of seeking you out again so that you might marry. Your mother, I believe, encouraged him to make his way here, so he might join them on their visit."

Temperance put one hand to her chest, her vision blurring as she tried to breathe but found it almost impossible to do so.

"Temperance, my dear." Her aunt rose and came across the room to sit with her, her hand going to her niece's cold one. "Are you all right? This must have come as a great shock, I understand, but it is good that Lord Calverton came to inform you of Lord Barlington's arrival."

Squeezing her eyes closed, Temperance let out a slow breath as she fought for relief, her whole body filled with a chill which seemed to seep down into her very bones. "I cannot believe he has come here," she whispered, opening her eyes to look at her aunt again. "To know that he is here, that he is nearby... what can my mother and father be thinking in encouraging his arrival?"

"Your mother is doing what she does," came the reply as Lady Hartford lifted and then dropped her shoulders. "She clearly believes that a reconciliation between the two of you is the very best thing."

A tear slid down Temperance's cheek. "But she does not understand my pain."

"No, she does not," Lady Hartford agreed, as Lord Calverton rose to his feet. "I am sorry to say that there is nothing that I can do to prevent this. If he arrives at the house and if your parents are both present and willing to receive him, then I will not be able to do anything to stop that."

Another tear fell to Temperance's cheek. "Then I will have to be in company with him?" she whispered, as her aunt nodded slowly. "I will have to *speak* with him?"

"I am sorry, Temperance." There came a slight tremble in her aunt's voice and Temperance's heart squeezed. Her aunt understood, wanted to do all she could to aid her but what could she do in this circumstance? It was clear that Lady Hartford *wanted* to be of aid to her and that was a comfort to Temperance all the same.

"I should take my leave." Lord Calverton inclined his head, his hands behind his back, his expression still serious. "I am sorry that I had such difficult news to impart, Lady Temperance."

Dashing one hand across her eyes to chase her tears away, Temperance rose quickly and reached out one hand to him, catching his fingers. "Please, do not apologise. I am truly grateful to you for coming to me and telling me of this. It means a great deal. To be told that this... this *gentleman* is going to be present here makes me both horrified and deeply saddened but had you not told me of it, had I been uninformed, then the shock would have been a good deal greater." She pressed his hand and then made to release it, only for Lord Calverton to press her fingers with his own again, and then bowed over her hand.

"I truly am a gentleman who keeps my word," he told her, standing tall and then releasing her hand. "Except in such circumstances as these, when I am not in the least bit inclined to do so!"

"I am grateful that you chose to do such a thing." Stepping back, Temperance felt herself wobble and chose to sit down again, albeit a little heavily. "Thank you, Lord Calverton."

He nodded, his eyes grave. "Will I see you this evening?"

Taking in a deep breath, Temperance lifted her chin and nodded. "Oh yes, Lord Calverton. I have no intention of permitting this news to prevent me from enjoying an evening in good company, particularly if it is going to be one of my *last* evenings to enjoy such company." Her voice faltered but she kept her gaze steady. "I will join you all as expected."

The smile which spread across Lord Calverton's face made her heart lift a little from the despair which pulled it low. "I am glad to hear that, Lady Temperance. Until this evening." He bowed and then turned to take his leave, just as Temperance turned to her aunt.

"I cannot quite take in what my mother thinks she is doing in hoping for a connection between Lord Barlington and myself," she said, as fresh tears burned in her eyes. "Surely she must understand how much pain that gentleman has brought to me!"

Her aunt shook her head. "I think, to be frank, that your mother supposes there is no-one else present who might marry you," she said, gently. "Therefore, she will push him towards you in the hope that he will propose and you will accept."

Temperance sighed heavily, managing to blink back her tears. "I daresay that elucidates the matter quite well," she said, heavily. "For what other gentleman *would* look at me? Who *would* consider someone as scarred and as broken as I?"

Her aunt's eyes flared wide. "Surely you do not mean to suggest that you will accept him?"

Immediately, Temperance shook her head. "No, of course not, Aunt. I only mean to say that I can now understand as to why my mother might think of such a thing. But no, I dread seeing him and I certainly shall not even consider accepting his attentions again." With a small sigh, she closed her eyes again. "What dreadful news this has been."

Chapter Ten

"Mother? Are you going to be ready to take our leave within the hour?" Doubts filled James' mind as he saw his mother press her brush back into the paints.

"Yes, yes. There is nothing much for me to do. I am already prepared and – "

"You have paint on your arm," James pointed out, coming closer to her as his mother looked down to see where he gestured. She then let out a breath of frustration before smiling rather ruefully. "It is only a little and the yellow goes with my gown, does it not?"

James let out a quiet chuckle and shook his head. "No, Mother, it does not go with your gown. It is clearly a daub of paint on the sleeve of your otherwise *dark blue* gown."

Much to his surprise, his mother only shrugged. "That does not matter to me very much. We are to be amongst friends and I do not think that they will have anything to say about it. Now," she continued, before he could protest, "what do you think of my painting?" She stepped back and permitted James to survey it and the landscape on the canvas quickly caught his breath.

It was a glorious sunset, with pink and orange streaks billowing across the sky. The dark greens and brown of the moorland was in sharp contrast but he could still see the red and yellow of the tiny little meadow flowers which she had painted into the scene. "Mother," he murmured, coming a little closer to it. "It is magnificent! You have a true skill."

His mother quickly shook her head. "No, I am not at all skillful. It has simply been practicing and practicing and practicing until I am happy with the result!"

James smiled softly and then, after a moment, kissed his mother's cheek. "I am delighted to see you painting again. You appear to be very happy indeed and that is a wonderful thing for me to see."

Lady Calverton looked up at him. "I do find it a blessing to be able to do such a thing as this. Though," she continued, her voice growing a little wistful, "the most beautiful stories are not painted on canvas but are written in the lines of our own lives." She tilted her head. "My life has known a great deal of pain and yet I find beauty and happiness in it still."

"That is because you are a remarkable lady," James answered her, stepping back so he could admire her artwork from a farther distance. "Now, as much as I should like to stand here and gaze at your painting for a little longer, I must go and prepare for this evening. You *will* be ready, will you not?"

His mother laughed and nodded. "Yes, of course I shall be. I am already looking forward to it."

His mind immediately went to Lady Temperance and James found himself smiling. "As am I, Mother. As am I."

***

"Billiards, my friend?"

James, who had been doing nothing other than watching Lady Thurston, Lady Temperance, Lady Hartford and his own mother playing cards for the last half an hour, smiled and rose to his feet. "Yes, of course." There came a slight reluctance to leave the ladies, to step away and to leave them behind, but he went there anyway. "I suppose I am doing nothing else!"

"Aside from watching the ladies, no, you are not." Lord Thurston grinned at him as they made their way into the billiards room. His smile faded as he turned his attention back towards James who was already picking up one of the cues. "Did you tell Lady Temperance about Lord Barlington's arrival?"

James nodded. "I did."

"And?"

"And she was stunned," James answered, approaching the table. "Horrified, in fact. I do not think I have ever seen anyone so utterly overwhelmed."

Lord Thurston clicked his tongue. "It is most displeasing to hear that he is forcing his return upon her."

"It is a little worse than that," James answered, shaking his head as his friend picked up the other cue. "Her mother appears to be in favour of it."

"In favour?" Lord Thurston's astonishment was evident in his wide eyes. "Goodness, whatever would she be in favour of it for? That gentleman caused her daughter a great deal of pain."

James shook his head. "I do not pretend to understand, my friend."

"That must pain the lady a great deal."

"I presume it does. You should have seen her expression when I told her that Lord Barlington had returned."

Lord Thurston tutted at the thought and then went to pour them both a snifter of brandy. "Here."

James accepted it with gladness. "I thank you."

"Might I ask you something?" Lord Thruston tilted his head as a cry of laughter rang through to them from the drawing room. "When it comes to Lady Temperance, might it be that there is a slight... interest there?"

James' eyebrows lifted. "Interest?"

"She intrigues you, does she not?"

"Intrigues me is perhaps not the right word for it," James answered, finding there to be no difficulty in telling his friend the truth. "I find her... remarkable."

Lord Thurston smiled. "My wife would agree with you there. She has endured such a great deal and yet she has not shied away entirely. Yes, she is a little reserved and it did take some time for her to trust Penelope and myself, but since that bond has been formed, Lady Temperance has spoken honestly to Penelope about a great many things. I know that her heart has been shattered not only by the accident but also by Lord Barlington's rejection of her. I also know – and I do not think that this is betraying a confidence – that her sisters showed her very little sympathy and her mother was quite insistent that she return to society once she was recovered."

James scowled "That speaks of a lack of understanding."

"Indeed. If it had not been for her aunt and her insistence that Lady Temperance should move here, I do not know what else the lady would have been forced to endure. To know now that Lord Barlington hopes that they will be able to resume their engagement does make me worry for the lady even more."

"As do I," James agreed, quietly. "She is happy this evening, but I fear that the happiness will not last long."

"Unless she finds another means of happiness," Lord Thurston suggested, a slight glint in his eye as he looked to James, one eyebrow arching. "If you truly find her remarkable then mayhap..."

James shook his head. "I do not know the lady very well as yet," he said, firmly. "For the moment, I am glad simply to be an acquaintance and though that is all I might ever be, I am still determined to do whatever I can to defend her – to protect her, if I must – from the likes of Lord Barlington and his no-doubt dark intentions."

Someone cleared their throat and James turned sharply, seeing none other than Lady Temperance standing there. Her cheeks were flushed, her eyes darting from one side of the room to the other as she clasped her hands in front of her, clearly a little embarrassed.

James closed his eyes and, after a moment, took a sip of his brandy simply so that he would not have to speak. How much had she overheard? How long had she been standing there?

"Lord Thurston, your wife begged me to tell you that we are quite ready for supper," she said, her voice very quiet indeed. "She would have come herself but it is her turn at whist."

"Of course," Lord Thurston answered, his gaze going to James who simply shrugged and then flushed hot as he caught Lady Temperance's glance. "We will be there in a trice. Thank you, Lady Temperance."

She smiled. "Of course." Her eyes slid towards James, the softness of her smile spreading a warmth across his heart and chasing away some of his embarrassment. "And thank you also, Lord Calverton."

He inclined his head though it was only when she left that he let out a long, slow breath, squeezing his eyes closed and shaking his head.

"I think she overheard the last of what you said, if that is what you are wondering," Lord Thurston said cheerfully, making James scowl. "But you did not say anything terrible and I am sure that she would have been rather pleased with what was said."

"Mayhap." James threw back the rest of his brandy and, picking up his cue, made towards the table. "I fully intend to beat you at billiards now, however, so that my confidence might be a little bolstered after such an embarrassment."

Lord Thurston chuckled and picked up his cue. "Very well, let us see if you can prove that... or if you will only add to your mortification."

Letting out a bark of laughter, James took his first shot and then grinned broadly at his friend. Lord Thurston rolled his eyes and then stepped forward, and the game commenced. All the same, however, James could not quite forget Lady Temperance's expression as she had looked back at him, as she had murmured that quiet, 'thank you'. Had she been pleased with what she had heard? Did she know just how strongly he felt in his desire to protect her? And more than that, was *he* truly aware of just how strong his own feelings were when it came to the lady?

Chapter Eleven

"Are you ready, Temperance?"

Temperance's stomach was churning so furiously, she felt as though she might cast up her accounts at the slightest provocation. "I do not think I can do this, Aunt."

"I know." Lady Hartford shook her head and then reached to squeeze Temperance's hand. "But be grateful that Lord Barlington himself is not present. You must consider this moment – and the conversation which is sure to follow – as the moment to make it quite plain to both your parents that you have no intention of seeking Lord Barlington's company again."

Temperance trembled violently. The arrival of her parents had been pleasant enough for she had been able to greet them and had spoken with them briefly before her mother and father had chosen to retire to their bedchamber. At breakfast, however, Temperance's mother had made it quite clear that there was something of significance that she wished to discuss with her – and though she had not given any specific statements as to what that might be, Temperance knew in her heart that it was about Lord Barlington. The time had now come for that conversation and try as she might, she could not find a way to escape it.

"Even the thought of speaking of him fills me with dread," she whispered, clutching her aunt's hand as she began to make her way to the drawing room. "I do not want to even mention him!"

"But mention him you must," her aunt replied, firmly. "I have already spoken to my sister. I have told her exactly what I think as regards this notion of hers and have made my feelings very plain indeed... but alas, I do not think that she will listen to me. *You must be strong, my dear. You must state quite clearly, that you have no intention of even being in the same room as Lord Barlington."

Temperance nodded, her nerves writhing as she stepped into the drawing room, her aunt close behind her. She managed a faint smile as her mother rose to her feet, coming across the room to take her daughter's hands.

"My dear girl, do come and sit down. Your father and I have been waiting for you." Her eyes flicked to her daughter's cheek and, much to Temperance's embarrassment, she turned her to one side, clearly gazing at the scar on her cheek. "That is still very severe, is it not?"

"It is not inclined to improve, Mama," Temperance answered, her face growing hot as she pulled her hands away from her mother's.

"There must be some creams or perhaps even poultices – "

"Tea, sister?" Lady Hartford stepped forward and gave Temperance a gentle smile, encouraging her to sit down and making her feel grateful that her aunt had interrupted her mother's questions and suggestions. No-one had looked at her scar with such an obvious eye in some time and Temperance recoiled from it, feeling shame bloom in her heart all over again.

"Thank you, Aunt," she murmured, as a cup of tea was set down before her. Daring a glance towards her father, Temperance let out a small sigh, seeing how his head lolled back as his eyes flickered closed. Evidently, he was not exactly eager to take part in this particular conversation. It seemed that this was just as her aunt had suspected; this notion of a healing between Temperance and Lord Barlington had been primarily her mother's idea.

"Now, Temperance." The Duchess smiled across the room at her though Temperance did not respond. "We have come to tell you some wonderful news!"

Temperance lifted her chin but kept her gaze steady. "Is that so?"

"Yes, indeed!" the Duchess exclaimed, before shooting a look towards her husband. Unfortunately, the Duke was now sound asleep and could not hear a single word which was being said to him. "Your father is clearly fatigued so therefore, I shall speak on his behalf. He is just as eager as I to tell you of this news!"

Temperance said nothing and instead, lifted her tea cup to take a sip, hoping that it would fortify her a little.

"The Marquess of Barlington came to call upon us recently," her mother continued, making Temperance tremble visibly. "He is greatly sorrowful about what happened. He regrets stepping away from you as he did and, in that, he now hopes that there can be a reconciliation between you."

Closing her eyes, Temperance shook her head.

"You will struggle to consider that, I understand," her mother continued, quickly, "but think about it practically,

Temperance! Lord Barlington is a gentleman with an excellent title, only one under the Dukedom of your father. He has a grand estate and is sure to have an excellent fortune. Why should you refuse to even consider him?"

"In case you have forgotten, Mama, that gentleman broke my heart," Temperance answered, hating that there was a slight tremble in her voice. "He turned away from me. He rejected me – and all because of my appearance. An accident injured me and yet he did not truly care about that. The only thing he desired was his own standing in society and thus, he stepped away from me without considering what I might feel because of that."

Her mother sighed and tutted lightly. "I am not saying that he did well, Temperance. However, he is clearly regretful and surely that is something which should be considered?"

"Considered?" Despite her best efforts, Temperance's anger flared. "Why should I consider him when he did not consider me? I am the one who is injured, I am the one who has been shamed by him and yet you ask me to consider the regret that *he* feels?"

"It does seem a little short sighted, Mary." Lady Hartford sat down and looked to her sister, her eyes sharp. "I do not know why you would insist upon such a thing."

The Duchess sighed heavily and looked away from Temperance, turning to Lady Hartford instead. "I am sure that you can understand it, should you be willing to *try* to think of it, my dear sister."

Temperance closed her eyes, already aware of what it was her mother was attempting to suggest. This was, as her aunt had thought, all about matrimony and Temperance's future. Clearly, her mother did not want to have a daughter unmarried, a daughter left to be a spinster, and thus, she thought that the only way forward was for her to return again to Lord Barlington's embrace.

The thought horrified her.

"My niece is happy here," Lady Hartford said, softly. "I am happy for her to remain here – to live here – for as long as she pleases."

"I *am* happy here," Temperance added, there was a slight wobble to her voice. "I do not think that anything needs to change. I am more than contented here. I have been able to recover from what happened, I have begun to heal from my emotional turmoil and I have been able to paint as often as I please. My dear Mama, surely you must be able to see that I am happy here... as happy as I can be. I do not want to even set eyes upon Lord Barlington! The thought has already distressed me a great deal."

Her mother clicked her tongue in obvious disappointment. "I think that is a great shame, Temperance."

A slight wave of relief washed over Temperance as she looked away from her mother. Was this to be the end of the conversation? Was it that she could be free from the suggestion that Lord Barlington be brought back into her life? Perhaps she had misjudged her mother. Mayhap she was going to listen to everything that she had said and choose not to press forward with this matter.

"I shall tell you something, Temperance, that may change your mind," the Duchess said, sitting forward in her chair and offering her daughter a warm smile which immediately pulled away the relief that had washed through Temperance only a moment ago. "Lord Barlington, in his regret and his sorrow, has chosen to come to join us here."

Temperance closed her eyes, letting out a slow breath. "Yes, Mama. I am aware that he has chosen to come to this area."

"He has *eschewed* society in order to come and be in company with you!" The Duchess exclaimed, her eyes flaring wide, her hands flinging either side. "Do you not understand? He has given up a great deal in order to come to see you, simply to express his regret and his deep sadness over what he has done!"

With a heaviness in her heart, Temperance shook her head. "That makes no difference to me."

"Well, it should!" her mother exclaimed, her eyes still wide. "He is a *marquess*! He is a gentleman who is eager to see you again *despite* what happened to you!"

Temperance's heart began to break all over again as her mother spoke. The lack of sympathy, of understanding and the clear push towards Lord Barlington made her want to either scream or cry, such was the pain within her. Her mother did not seem to care about what she thought. The only thing she wanted was for her daughter to become a married lady and the only way that she could do that was to press her back towards the very gentleman who had caused her an unspeakable amount of pain.

"I think that you should listen to your mother."

Blinking back fresh tears, Temperance looked to her father who, having seemingly been asleep, now shifted in his chair and cracked open one eye to look at her.

"I have spoken to Lord Barlington at length and I understand that he is truly sorry for his actions. You must understand, my dear girl, that I was not at all inclined towards hearing a word he had to say but, after your mother came to me with her thoughts on the matter, I decided that I should listen to him. That is all we are asking of you at present, Temperance. We are not stating that you *must* accept his offer of courtship, when it is given, nor are we saying that you should begin to consider matrimony. All we are asking is that you let him speak to you. Is that truly so much to ask?"

"Yes," Temperance whispered, only for her mother to interject.

"Then it is settled! Temperance, you know very well that it is expected of you to do as your father states. Therefore, I will send a note to Lord Barlington and tell him to come to call tomorrow afternoon – or at his earliest convenience."

Yet again, tears sprang into Temperance's eyes but rather than let them fall, rather than let them dash down to her cheeks and let her mother see her in such a state of upset, she simply rose to her feet, excused herself and quit the room.

Within a few minutes, she was outside, walking hurriedly along the path to the clifftops, her tears now flowing furiously and yet being whipped away by the wind. Her heart was so painful, it was almost too difficult to breathe, her hands curling into fists as she fought to keep ahold of herself.

I am going to have to see him again, she realized, her chest tight with sadness and anger. *I am going to have to endure him speaking with me, hearing him telling me of his regret and his upset. I will have to look him in the eye and see my mother's encouraging smile just behind him. And I will feel myself broken all over again.*

"Lady Temperance?"

Temperance dashed her tears with the back of her hand, seeing two figures come towards her. The first she recognized to be Lord Thurston, the gentleman calling her name, and the other with him was Lord Calverton. Her heart leapt suddenly though she quickly forced it quiet. Somehow, seeing him made her difficulty with Lord Barlington seem a little less.

"Good afternoon." She offered a small smile but didn't quite manage to meet their gaze, wondering if her eyes were a little red. "Are you enjoying your walk?"

Lord Calverton nodded. "Yes, we are." There was a hint of concern in his voice as he took a small step closer. "Are you quite all right, Lady Temperance? Is something the matter?"

She did not know what to say. She looked up into his eyes, holding his gaze steadily. Dare she tell both Lord Thurston and himself the truth about her present feelings? Or would it be best to keep all of this to herself?

Chapter Twelve

To James' mind, Lady Temperance looked rather distraught. Her bonnet was slightly askew, her eyes darting here and there and he could not help but notice how she squeezed her hands together and then released them over and over again.

"Are you quite all right, Lady Temperance? Is something the matter?"

He could tell from the way that she bit her lip that she was uncertain as to whether or not to share with him whatever had taken place. Lord Thurston glanced at him and James offered a slight shrug.

"I think I shall take a walk down to the shore," Lord Thurston said, with a small smile in Lady Temperance's direction. "Do excuse me."

"Should you like to join us?" James asked, turning just a little to offer her his arm. "If you like, you would be very welcome to take a short walk and I can promise you I will not ask you any more questions, should you have no desire to speak."

Lady Temperance took his arm with a small smile and James' heart turned over on itself as he walked alongside her. Lord Thurston continued to walk a few steps ahead of them both and as they walked, James heard the long, sorrowful sigh which came from Lady Temperance. He had to clamp his mouth shut for fear that he would begin to do the very thing he had promised he would not do; namely to ask her what the trouble was.

"I want to thank you again for what you did in informing me of Lord Barlington's arrival." Lady Temperance glanced up at him as they approached the steps and the path which would take them down to the shore. "My mother and father are insisting that I speak with him. Indeed, my mother is insisting that I consider him, in fact."

James' eyebrows lifted. "Consider him?" he repeated, as Lady Temperance nodded. "You mean to say that – " Embarrassed at his own lack of control, James clamped his mouth shut and gave her a slight shake of his head. "Forgive me."

"It is quite all right. I would be telling Lady Thurston of it all and, no doubt, you would hear of it soon enough." She sighed again and looked away from him. "My mother is most insistent that I think about engaging myself to Lord Barlington again. She thinks that the best suggestion as regards my future would be to consider marrying the very gentleman who broke my heart by his rejection and betrayal."

"I can imagine that the thought of that is a very displeasing one."

She looked up at him, her face a little flushed, her eyes blinking rapidly. "It is. The reason you find me out walking at this time – and in something of a flustered state – is because my own considerations were not listened to. My mother and father both insist that I am to consider Lord Barlington again, that I have no other choice but to do so. I have protested, I have told them what I feel and why my inclination is set entirely against him but the choice has been taken from me."

Anger began to lick up James' heart but he kept himself steady rather than responding in any way. Why would any parent force such a thing upon their daughter? He himself did not know Lady Temperance very well as yet but even *he* could see how much she was troubled by this. He could not imagine the pain that she was enduring, having already dealt with a great deal.

"And thus, Lord Barlington is going to call very soon and I will be expected not only to tolerate his presence but also to listen to him as he expresses various sentiments – none of which I want to listen to. It seems that both he and my parents are entirely unaware that I am contented just as I am." Her gaze grew rather wistful as she looked out across the ocean, her expression softening. "The last two years, I have become very happy here. I have found myself free rather than trapped. There is a contentedness within me which I did not expect to find and I do not want to be pulled away from it. My mother may not like that it appears I am to be a spinster but what of my own feelings?"

James' stomach dropped low and he swallowed hard, suddenly a little distressed at hearing the satisfaction of which she spoke. Was she truly happy at being a spinster? Did she not desire anything more?

"I do not think I will be able to express such a thing to Lord Barlington, however," Lady Temperance continued, as James fought to control his own emotions and simply listen to her. "He will be more interested in telling me about his own feelings rather than listen to my own." Her eyes closed tightly and James' heart twisted with sympathy. "I will not be able to say anything to him, I will be forced only to listen. No doubt he will offer a great many words to try and convince me, to almost demand that I accept what he has to say."

"Mayhap I could help?" James saw how her eyebrows lifted, but then pressed on. "If you knew of when he was to call, then mayhap my mother and I might come to call at the very same time? It would mean that he would be interrupted and mayhap, you would not have to endure for so very long?"

After a moment, Lady Temperance smiled and James found himself smiling back as they finally stepped out onto the beach.

"Would you truly do such a thing for me?"

"I would, of course I would. And I am certain that my mother would be very glad to call upon you again and should Lord and Lady Thurston know of this visit also, then I am certain they would join us also! It could be an unexpected visit *but* it would also show Lord Barlington that you have friends here, that you are well connected and do not require *his* company."

Lady Temperance's smile grew bigger, though her eyes glistened gently. "That would be quite wonderful. I would not have thought about such a thing myself."

"Then shall we tell Lord Thurston?"

With a nod, Lady Temperance called to Lord Thurston and, turning, the gentleman came to join them again post-haste. Without hesitation, Lady Temperance began to explain what had happened, ending by asking Lord Thurston if he and his wife might join James to call almost at the very same time.

Lord Thurston, just as James had known he would, agreed at once.

"I should be very glad to do so," Lord Thurston said quickly, as James offered him a small smile. "And I know that Penelope will want to do the very same thing."

Lady Temperance let out a slow breath but this time, she was smiling. "This has made me feel a great deal better. Thank you. Thank you both."

"But of course." James smiled back at her. "Will you write a note to either Lady Thurston or to myself so that we know when to call?"

"I will write to you both," came the reply. "Thank you, Lord Thurston, thank you, Lord Calverton." Her eyes closed briefly, her smile faltering a little. "While this may be a very difficult situation, it is already a little easier knowing that my friends will be there."

James' heart lifted as Lord Thurston responded with encouraging words. Yes, he thought to himself, I *am* Lady Temperance's friend.

The question which came next made his heart twist, his brows furrowing with uncertainty.

What if he wanted to be something more?

***

"You are not eating, my son."

James looked up at his mother, having been entirely lost in thought. "I am sorry, Mother, I did not hear what you said."

She smiled at him, her eyes twinkling. "I said that you are not eating but evidently, you are not listening to me either!"

A slight heat touched James' cheeks. "I am sorry. My thoughts are... elsewhere."

"Oh?"

The edge of James' lip lifted. "Mother, we are going to call on Lady Hartford and Lady Temperance tomorrow. Though I am not certain what time we are to call as yet."

Light lit up his mother's features. "How wonderful!"

"That is why I am caught up in my thoughts," James explained. "Lady Temperance is in something of a difficulty. Her mother and father have come to reside with Lady Hartford, but they have also brought another guest with them, though he is not residing in the same place."

"And who is this guest?"

James closed his eyes for a moment, still barely able to believe that the Duke and Duchess were so blind to their daughter's suffering. "The Marquess of Barlington intends to come to call upon Lady Temperance, desiring to speak of his regret and sorrow over what he did in separating and ending their engagement."

There was nothing but silence for a few moments. James looked back at his mother, seeing the slight twitch of her lips, noting the darkness which flashed in her eyes and understanding that she now felt the very same way as he.

"How utterly... !" Lady Calverton's expression scrunched into one of anger. "That is ridiculous. That poor girl! How injured she must be knowing that is the gentleman's intention! Whyever would the Duke of Danfield permit that gentleman back into her sphere?"

"I do not know."

"Ah." Lady Calverton closed her eyes, shaking her head. "Of course."

James' eyebrows lifted as he waited for his mother to explain.

"He will think – as will his wife – that no other gentleman would consider her given her injury. And thus, if the Marquess has shown an interest in the lady again, then they will consider it best that their connection is reformed. That way, Lady Temperance would be married and settled and would not be a spinster which, of course, the Duke – or mayhap, the Duchess – might consider something of an embarrassment."

"Lady Temperance's happiness does not seem to matter one whit," James muttered, finding his anger returning. "Mother, I spoke to Lady Temperance about this situation earlier today. We happened upon each other and it was decided that not only the two of us but also Lord and Lady Thurston would all arrive at Lady Hartford's residence at the very same time as Lord Barlington comes to call. Lady Hartford will be made aware of this plan, I am sure, but the Duke and Duchess – and Lord Barlington himself, of course – will not be. You understand our intention, I am sure!"

"To disrupt Lord Barlington's visit with Lady Temperance, thereby bringing her relief," his mother said, with a firm nod. "Of *course* I understand. I am glad to help."

"Good. I thank you."

"You are aware that your consideration of Lady Temperance is growing, are you not?"

The quiet question made James frown. "It is not something that should be a surprise, I should think. Every gentleman, every lady with a kind heart would see her in the very same way as I."

"Though mayhap without the edge of affection?"

James blinked and then let his brows drop low. "Mother, please. While I am aware that I must marry and preserve the family line, you cannot think that I would then pursue Lady Temperance, someone who has been left broken-hearted and deeply pained by the behaviour of another gentleman? It is clear to me that the young lady requires friendship and support rather than the pursuit of affection."

His mother only smiled and James, a little frustrated that she had been able to see something within his actions which he himself had been unable to hide from her – and evidently, from himself as well – let out a heavy sigh.

"Please, do not make such connections in your thoughts, Mother," he said, firmly. "My only desire is to aid Lady Temperance in any way I can, to make her life a little happier than it is at present."

"And what if your heart begins to hold a little more affection for her than you had expected?" she asked, quietly. "Surely there can be nothing wrong in pursuing a young lady such as she?"

James shook his head. "It is clear from what she said this afternoon that she is more than contented as she is. I believe she stated, quite clearly, that she is happy to be a spinster, to live with her aunt and her uncle and – "

"That is because she believes that no gentleman would ever look at her and consider her as a lady ought to be considered," Lady Calverton interrupted, sharply. "Do you not see that, Calverton?"

James tilted his head. "Mayhap," he remarked, softly. "But for the moment, my only desire is to aid her. That is all that I want."

"Very good." His mother smiled. "Then have no doubt, I will be alongside you in every respect. Lady Temperance will be saved from Lord Barlington... and Lord Barlington will not know what to do with himself by the time I am finished with him!"

Chuckling softly, James lifted a glass in his mother's direction. "I look forward to seeing it, Mother," he replied, seeing her grin. "Until tomorrow, then."

Chapter Thirteen

It was difficult indeed to stop herself trembling but Temperance forced herself to sit still and, clasping her hands tight together, kept her chin lifted as Lord Barlington was introduced.

She kept her gaze steady, silently demanding that she look at him though she did not rise to her feet to greet him.

Her mother's angry glare caught her attention but Temperance did not move. Much to her relief, her aunt barely got to her feet before she sat back down again, taking her place beside Temperance in obvious solidarity.

"How very good of you to permit me into this house." Lord Barlington bowed low in Lady Hartford's direction, his hand reaching out to her as though to beseech her all the more, though Lady Hartford remained where she was and did not move an inch. "And you, Lady Temperance, how grateful I am to you for your willingness to see me."

Temperance lifted her eyes to his, taking in Lord Barlington's handsome face. It was unmarred, his brown hair flopping over dark brown eyes... and yet her heart remained unmoved. Her chest grew tight, her hands clasping hard as she swallowed at the knot in her throat. Lord Barlington's eyes went to her cheek, his gaze tracing the scar which ran down one side of her face.

Temperance's face grew hot but she did not move. Her scar was something he had seen before and she fully expected him to turn away from it in the same way he had done before.

She was not disappointed. His eyes pulled quickly from her face and he cleared his throat.

Rather than squirm, Temperance forced herself to speak, her words brittle but honest. "I did not desire to see you, Lord Barlington," she answered, her voice hoarse and broken. "This meeting is not at all my desire. Do not think that I had any say in the matter."

"Temperance!" The Duchess got to her feet at once, her eyes filled with fire, her hands flung wide. "How can you say such a thing?"

Temperance looked back at her mother steadily, having already decided – both within her own heart and in conversation with her aunt – that she would be entirely truthful in this circumstance, no matter what was said. "Mother, I have no interest in being in Lord Barlington's company. It is yourself and father who have asked me to do this and it is for that reason and that reason alone that I have agreed... nay, have been forced into doing this."

"That is quite enough. Lord Barlington, I do apologise." The Duchess gestured for him to sit down and, though her father was not present, from the angry look which her mother sent her, Temperance understood that he would be informed of what she had done.

She did not care.

"It is more than understandable and please, do not think that I expected anything less." Rather than take his leave, as Temperance had hoped for, Lord Barlington sat down close to her and, with a scowl, she turned her head away from him. "I did not think for a moment that Lady Temperance would be glad to see me. That is, as I have said, perfectly understandable."

Temperance kept her head turned away, seeing her aunt roll her eyes and finding her trembling beginning to dissipate completely. With her aunt's company and obvious dislike of Lord Barlington's presence, she felt her courage rising just a little. She was not required to offer Lord Barlington anything and certainly did not have to give him even a single moment of her attention if she did not wish it.

Her hands softened in her lap and she took in a slow breath, letting her thoughts turn to her other friends. Lord and Lady Thurston, Lord Calverton and his mother would soon be joining them and though her mother was not expecting them, her aunt was and that would bring an even greater distraction to Lord Barlington's company and conversation.

"I do not have to stay for long, though I would very much like to speak with you, Lady Temperance." Lord Barlington's voice grew soft, a tenderness there which made her lip curl, her dislike of his presence growing all the more. "I know that I have done you a great wrong and I should very much like to have the opportunity to speak to you of my regret."

"I am sure that my daughter will be willing to give you such a thing," her mother said, before Temperance could offer a single word. "Would you like to speak with her now? I am sure that my sister and I could step to the back of the room for a time and – "

"Where is that tea tray?" Lady Hartford got to her feet, marching across the room to ring the bell, only to come back and sit back down purposefully beside Temperance. "Where is it that you are residing, Lord Barlington?"

Temperance reached across and pressed her aunt's hand in what she hoped was a surreptitious manner. She did not want to be forced into staying in Lord Barlington's presence and hearing him speak! She knew very well that her mother and father were eager for a reconciliation – her mother more than her father – but to press this onto her at their very first meeting was more than Temperance would have been able to bear. Clearly, her aunt had recognized that. *If only my mother had too.*

"I am residing in Lord Grayson's manor house, which is only four or five miles from here." Lord Barlington smiled as though this was something that Temperance ought to be delighted about but she turned her head away again, only to catch her mother's angry glare. With an effort, she ignored it, letting her gaze rest against the wall at the back of the room rather than looking at her mother or at Lord Barlington.

"I see. I am acquainted with Lord Grayson, of course, but not particularly well. He only resides here on occasion."

"Yes, that is so. He does spend a great deal of time in London," came the reply, just as a knock came at the door. Lady Hartford called for the maid to enter and a tea tray was brought in.

"Temperance," her mother said crisply. "Might you pour the tea? Thereafter, I am sure that your aunt and I can give both Lord Barlington and yourself a few minutes to speak."

Temperance opened her mouth to say that she had no desire to sit and listen to Lord Barlington, only for a knock to come to the door again. She caught her aunt's eye and saw a smile cross her aunt's face; the very same smile which came to her own lips.

"Do come in," her aunt called, and the door opened to reveal Lord and Lady Thurston, quickly followed by Lord Calverton and his mother.

Relief poured through Temperance like water rushing over her and she could not help but sigh gently as she smiled.

"Ah, an unexpected visit!" Lady Hartford cried, throwing up her hands in seeming delight. "Another tea tray, Jenkins, of course. Please, do come in!"

"Oh, but we are interrupting!" Lady Thurston did not pause in her entrance but came quickly towards Temperance, smiling at her as she spoke. "I must apologise. It was such a miserable afternoon and I was finding myself rather dulled – and then my dear husband suggested that we come to call on you both, only to find that you have company."

Lady Hartford beamed at them both. "That is quite all right. How glad I am to see you both!"

"And I was quite determined to speak to you, Lady Temperance, about your artwork," Lady Calverton added, sitting down in a chair without waiting for any sort of introduction. "I insisted that my son bring us here at once, for I was certain that you would not have stepped outside in such weather as this!"

Temperance glanced to the window, seeing the raindrops tumbling down. "Indeed," she smiled, sitting down quickly. "I am very glad to see you again. Of course, we may speak of whatever you wish."

"Though mayhap someone should make some introductions?"

Glancing to her mother, whose tone had dropped somewhat as she sent uncertain glances from one person to the next, Temperance gestured to her aunt. "Aunt? Might you be willing to do so?"

"But of course." Quickly, Lady Hartford introduced everyone and though some smiles were given and though Lord Calverton and Lord Thurston bowed, there was a clear coldness offered to Lord Barlington. Whether or not Lord Barlington noticed it, Temperance did not know, but all the same she found herself very grateful indeed for their presence. The second tea tray was brought in and Temperance let herself settle back a little more into her chair. She was quite certain that Lord Barlington would attempt to call again, would try to offer his explanation for what he had done at another time but she could not let herself think of that at this present moment. There was enough of a relief here for her to settle into, knowing that there was going to be nothing more that Lord Barlington could do to force her into speaking with him. No doubt her mother would be frustrated but Temperance could not let herself be concerned with that.

"Might I ask if you are well acquainted with Lady Temperance and Lady Hartford?"

Temperance's head lifted as she caught the slight frown flickering across Lord Barlington's forehead as he asked such a question, looking to Lord Calverton as he spoke.

"I would say that we are fairly well acquainted, yes," came the reply as Lord Calverton offered Temperance a small smile. "It has been a very pleasant experience becoming all the better acquainted also, I would say. Would you not agree, Mother?"

"Certainly I would!" Lady Calverton agreed, quickly. "Lady Temperance and I have a great deal in common when it comes to our painting."

Lord Barlington blinked. "Painting?"

"Yes, of course." Lady Calverton looked rather surprised. "Do you not know how wonderful an artist is Lady Temperance?"

A small silence spread across the room and, though she was a little embarrassed, Temperance kept her expression as calm as she could, seeing how Lord Barlington frowned.

"No, I was unaware that Lady Temperance had such a gift."

Lady Thurston laughed softly, catching everyone's attention. "Then you cannot have known her very well when you were connected, Lord Barlington," she said, making Lord Barlington's frown deepen though Temperance's heart lifted at the way her friends were coming together to support her. "Mayhap you were not particularly interested in that sort of connection, however? Although that, again, is a loss that you must bear. There is a great deal of worth and wonder in Lady Temperance's character and abilities. That is why I count myself as very fortunate indeed to be her friend."

Temperance smiled warmly as Lady Thurston finished, seeing her friend give her a small nod as she took in all that had been said. There was such a sweetness to Lady Thurston's words that even in the company of Lord Barlington, Temperance felt herself entirely at ease. This was showing Lord Barlington that not only did she have friends, but she had *dear* friends, those who valued her for who she was, even with the scar to her face. No-one here had rejected her, no-one had turned their back on her and sent her away. How much she hoped that Lord Barlington could see the difference between their words and his actions!

"It seems that I have a great deal still to learn – and still to appreciate – about Lady Temperance," Lord Barlington murmured, making Temperance's spine stiffen straight away.

She picked up her tea cup and brought it to her lips, refusing to look at the gentleman.

"It seems to me as though you may have already had that opportunity, have you not?" Lord Calverton's voice held a dark tone to it, a severity which made Temperance's lips curve into a small, satisfied smile as she looked across the room at him, seeing how he had pinned a rather fierce gaze upon Lord Barlington.

"That is quite true." Lord Barlington's shoulders lifted, his face a little flushed as he looked across to Temperance, though she made certain to lift her tea cup to her lips rather than look back at him. "Though, if I am fortunate, I may be given another opportunity."

Without having had any intention of doing so, Temperance snorted gently, only for her face to flush hot as every eye turned towards her. She took another sip of her tea as her aunt quickly suggested that everyone take something more to eat from the tea tray. Try as she might, Temperance could not remove the heat from her cheeks though, as she looked across the room and caught Lady Thurston's eye, she saw the smile there and found herself wanting to burst out into laughter.

"At least you made yourself clear," her aunt murmured, as Lady Calverton began to speak at length with Temperance's mother, asking about her residence and her situation there. "It is not something to be embarrassed about, my dear. Lord Barlington appears to believe that he is more than able simply to march back into your life and have you practically on your knees before him in gratitude at his return! Your friends and your own response to him have made it very clear that it will not be so."

Temperance gave her aunt a smile. "Thank you, Aunt. And thank you for agreeing to their arrival at the very same time as Lord Barlington."

"But of course!"

"Alas," Temperance continued, seeing her mother smile at Lady Calverton, though it was not a smile that spread wide, "I do not think that my mother is pleased."

Her aunt shrugged. "It does not matter whether she is pleased or not, does it? This has been forced upon you and you are not required to be contented with it."

Temperance's heart squeezed and she took a moment to let her aunt's words sink in. "That is true, I suppose."

"And you will have me to defend you when your mother decides to berate you for this afternoon," Lady Hartford continued, firmly. "You are not alone in this, Temperance. Look around you! You are *never* alone."

With a smile, Temperance reached to squeeze her aunt's hand, her heart aching softly. In this room, with her friends – both new and old – she was *not* alone, left to face Lord Barlington without support or defense... and that realization brought her the greatest of encouragements.

Chapter Fourteen

"I think the plan went very well indeed."

James lifted his shoulders and then let them fall as he and Lord Thurston rode along the path to the small village. "I do not think that Lord Barlington has been at all dissuaded, however."

"Does that matter?" Lord Thurston tilted his head. "It seems to me that Lady Temperance was relieved that we were present and that should be the only thing that matters, should it not?"

James considered this and then nodded. "Yes, I suppose so."

"But you feel differently?"

With a small hesitation, James chose to be honest about his own heart. "I am concerned that Lord Barlington will not give up and that troubles me a great deal. I understand that Lady Temperance was relieved yesterday but what if Lord Barlington should try again? What if he should come upon her deliberately when we are not present? I saw in her eyes how distressed she was just as we arrived."

"And that pained your heart."

James looked to his friend. "Did it not pain yours?"

Lord Thurston nodded. "Of course. Though mayhap without the same intensity that you feel at present."

Scowling, James looked away from Lord Thurston, keeping his gaze towards the path. "You sound like my mother."

"You mean that both she and I are stating the very same thing, albeit in a slightly hidden manner?" Lord Thurton chuckled softly. "Yes, my friend. I think that you are beginning to have a greater consideration for Lady Temperance than you would wish to admit."

James shrugged again. "Be that as it may – and no, you need not lift your eyebrows at me like that for I am well aware I have told you the truth without hesitation – Lady Temperance has made it quite clear that she desires only to be as she is at present. When I spoke with her, she stated that her father and mother do not see that she is contented as she is. Who am I to push myself forward into that? If she is happy, then I have no desire to alter that happiness in any way."

Lord Thurston frowned. "But she may not even think that you are considering her in that way. It may be that she cannot even imagine a gentleman having any sort of interest in her! I do not think that I am speaking out of turn to say that I know for certain that such a situation is not something that Lady Temperance has ever considered."

His mother's words came back to him with force as James considered what his friend had said. That was the second time he had heard that Lady Temperance would never even consider that a gentleman might look at her in such a way! Would she be happy to know that *he* was beginning to feel a flicker of affection towards her?

"It is not as though she is going to accept Lord Barlington's interest," Lord Thurston continued, as they made their way into the village. "Quite what that gentleman hopes to achieve by coming here, I do not know."

"Nor do I," James agreed, "though my mind is a little troubled. I worry that there is something a little more nefarious at play here."

Lord Thurston looked at him sharply. "Oh?"

"This is something I considered only this morning," James told his friend. "Why is Lord Barlington come to pursue Lady Temperance? He ended their engagement yes, and certainly the *ton* might think rather poorly of him – though some, I think, would say that they understood and agreed with his decision. Therefore, why would he not then be able to pursue *another* young lady? What is it about Lady Temperance that pulls him so quickly towards her?"

There was a slight pause. "She is the daughter of a Duke, I suppose."

"Yes, but he is a Marquess. There is no disappointment in that. Besides which, if he *were* to marry Lady Temperance, he would have whispers and the like follow after him for many a year. Not that I think such a thing is right, of course."

"Of course not, but what you are saying is true." Lord Thurston's brows knotted. "That must mean that there is some reason, some purpose, in what he is doing."

"Precisely."

"And you would like to find out what that is?"

James pursed his lips, considering. "I am not certain," he answered, after a few moments as they made their way into the village. "It is not my place, so I do not know whether I ought to do such a thing or not."

"Yes, but you are her friend, as am I and as is my wife," came the response. "I think it would be wise for us to discuss this all with Lady Temperance and see what she thinks."

James found himself nodding. "Yes, I should like to do that."

"Good." Jumping down from his horse, Lord Thurston gestured to the tavern across the street from where they were at present. "Should you like to go and join the locals for a quick drink?"

James chuckled and dismounted, throwing the reins to a young lad, along with a coin and the promise that they would return within the hour and that more coin would follow, should he look after their horses well. He stepped out with Lord Thurston, knowing that the locals would give them their very best table but, at the same time, be pleased to know that two gentlemen of the *ton* had chosen to come and sit in their establishment. He had no doubt that it was not the first time Lord Thurston had frequented this place and it would not be the last.

Pushing open the door, he soon had himself seated at a table in the corner of the room, right next to a very large window. It was a little grubby, so difficult to make out everything clearly, but all the same, he appreciated it. Lord Thurston sat down with two glasses in his hands and, with a grin, James took one from him.

"I thank you." He studied the glass, a little surprised at how clean it was. "This place is quite satisfactory, is it not?"

Lord Thurston grinned. "It is! I have come here alone at times and always found it quite pleasant in fact! Though the local folk do not come and converse with me, I will say. In that regard, I am a little too high for them though I should not be displeased if they came to speak! I would be glad of conversation, I think."

"At least you have conversation now," James chuckled, only to catch sight of a figure walking towards the establishment. His brow immediately lowered, his shoulders dropping. "Though we may not be able to stay for too long. I believe that Lord Barlington intends to step into this very place!"

Lord Thurston's eyebrows lifted. "Lord Barlington?"

James nodded, not able to say more as the gentleman pushed open the door and stepped inside. James turned his face away at once, Lord Thurston rounding his shoulders a little as though that might hide his profile from the gentleman. Much to James' relief, however, Lord Barlington simply went straight to the barman, requested a drink and, thereafter, walked across the room to sit down on the opposite side of the tavern.

James let out a small breath of relief. "I do not think that he saw us."

"It is very unusual for a gentleman of his ilk to come and sit in here alone, however," Lord Thurston remarked, glancing across the room towards the man in question. "A Marquess in a tavern, in a small village such as this? Why ever should he do that?"

"And he does live some miles away also," James muttered, lifting his glass to his lips. "That is a little unusual."

Lord Thurston shrugged. "Mayhap he is doing his best to show Lady Temperance that he is a gentleman willing to do whatever he must to fit into this place she has come to love. Mayhap she hopes that the villagers will speak well of him and that she will hear of that in some way."

James' lip curled. "Mayhap." He threw another glance at the gentleman, only for his eyebrows to lift. "Look. There is someone coming to speak with him."

Lord Thurston turned to look. "Indeed there is."

"Do you recognise him?"

His friend shook his head. "I do not."

James let himself study the interaction, his eyebrows lifting as the man slammed one fist down on the table, only for Lord Barlington to rise up out of his chair, plant his hands on the table and glare at the fellow in return. "There is an argument, certainly."

"Though that fellow does not appear to be one of the high gentry."

"No, he does not." James tilted his head just a little, observing the fellow. "A knight or a baron, mayhap? I wonder what such a person has to do with the Marquess."

"I do not know but there is clearly something that has frustrated him. The Marquess has only been here for a few days, how could it be that there is something so significant between this other fellow and himself so quickly?"

A sense of uncertainty wrapped around James' heart and he shook his head. "I do not know. Though I confess that I should be very interested in finding out."

Lord Thurston chuckled darkly. "As would I. It is not a fair consideration, I know, for a gentleman's business ought to be his own but given his intention as regards Lady Temperance, a lady whom my wife and I consider to be a very dear friend, I think the urge is only right."

James nodded and continued to watch as the fellow glared back at Lord Barlington, only to slam his fist on the table again, say something more to him and then turn to walk out of the tavern.

"I will go after him," Lord Thurston said quickly, rising to his feet. "I am known around here so it will not bring any sort of suspicion if I speak to this fellow, whoever he is."

"Do not ask anything too obvious," James warned, only for Lord Thurston to nod and then step away. Despite the urge to continue to watch Lord Barlington, James forced his gaze away and kept it on the window, seeing the outline of Lord Thurston as he approached the other fellow. The man did stop and bowed towards Lord Thurston, before they lingered in conversation. James bit his lip, watching them speak and wondering just what it was that Lord Thurston was asking him. It was all rather strange. Seeing the man step away, he waited for a moment, only for Lord Thurston to beckon to him through the window. Getting up out of his chair, James threw back the rest of his drink and then made his way to the door, managing one sidelong glance towards Lord Barlington. Relieved that the gentleman had not noticed him, he stepped outside into the sunshine and to where Lord Thurston was.

"That was Sir Jeffries," Lord Thurston said, the moment James came to meet him. "He is not high in the gentry, as I suspected, but we are acquainted. I did not recognise him until we came outside and, of course, I pretended surprise at meeting him here."

"And did he say why he was present?" James asked, as the two made their way directly across the street and away from the tavern. "Did he mention Lord Barlington?"

Lord Thurston shook his head. "No, he did not and I did not pry. I did not think that it would be wise to do so. Instead, I simply asked about his family and situation and he told me that his presence here in the village was on matters of business... and because his daughter insisted on going to the haberdashery."

James' lips pursed. "I see."

"We have not learned anything useful, only to say that Lord Barlington and Sir Jeffries are somehow acquainted."

"And that there is bad feeling between them for some reason," James added, turning around to survey the tavern. "It is very strange indeed. I should like to ask Lord Barlington about it just to see what he would say but I do not think it would be wise. If he is attempting to hide something, then asking him questions will not help."

"No, it will not. Instead, I think it would force him to stay even quieter."

James looked to his friend. "Then what shall we do?"

After a moment, Lord Thurston nodded to himself and then looked to James. "I think that we should say nothing and do nothing for the moment. It would not be wise to say anything to anyone else – including Lady Temperance – since we have no proof of anything."

"But I must do something!"

Lord Thurston nodded. "Of course. Might I suggest that we then agree to observe Lord Barlington as best we can? Speak with him, encourage an acquaintance between us? It may be that more of such behaviour appears and we will be able to discover something more."

A scowl darkened James' features once more. "Then that means I shall have to engage in conversation with him, pretend that I find his company a delight rather than unwelcome." A sudden thought hit him and he shook his head. "I cannot do that, not when Lady Temperance will believe that – "

"Then inform her of what you are doing but do not say any more than that," his friend interrupted, gently. "Mayhap you merely say that you are looking to make certain of Lord Barlington's motivations and thus, you think it best to make certain of his movements about the area. You need not explain any more than that."

James nodded. "An excellent suggestion," he agreed, feeling himself a little more assured. "I shall do that." His eyes flared as he caught sight of his carriage approaching. "Goodness, it appears as though my mother is determined to join us today! She was muttering about coming in search of various things for her artwork here in the village."

Lord Thurston's eyebrows lifted. "I did not think that such a small place would have such things."

"She has had some things sent here from town, I believe." James smiled as Lord Thurston nodded his understanding. "On the very day that my mother picked up her paintbrush again, she sent various letters to town and the like, determined to have the very best of supplies sent back to her."

"Ah." Lord Thurston chuckled. "Then do you wish to join her?"

"I suppose I should," James grinned. "Though do not feel as though you have to stay."

Lord Thurston made to say something, only to open his eyes a little wider as he looked beyond the approaching carriage. "Though that appears to be my very own carriage coming also!"

"Your wife?" James asked, as Lord Thurston nodded. "Then it seems we are both to stay!" With a smile, he waited for the carriage to arrive, all thought of Lord Barlington – for the moment, at least – gone from his mind.

Chapter Fifteen

"A very fine afternoon, is it not?"

Temperance smiled at her friend as the carriage made its way into the village. She knew very well what Lady Thurston was doing and she appreciated it a great deal. "Yes, it is very fine."

"And it is a blessing to be able to escape from the confines of the house, is it not?" Lady Thurston chuckled as Temperance laughed along with her. "I can imagine that it is not a particularly encouraging situation at your aunt's house at the moment."

The smile faded from Temperance's face. "Indeed, it has been rather trying. My mother was greatly displeased with what happened at our first meeting with Lord Barlington, though she did also attempt to blame my aunt for that."

Lady Thurston's eyebrows lifted. "Really? I would imagine that your aunt did not respond well to such a thing!"

That brought a smile back to Temperance's face. "Indeed, she did not. My aunt responded with such a sharpness that I believe that my mother was rather surprised! Though it did take the weight from my shoulders a little, which I was grateful for."

"Though Lord Barlington is going to continue in his determinations to speak with you, is he not?"

Temperance let out a slow sigh. "Yes, I presume that he will."

"Well, I shall have to come to call a good deal more often – or to insist that you come out in the carriage with me as we are doing at this present moment," her friend replied, firmly. "I know we are only going to the village but it is enough to take up a few hours."

"Yes, indeed it is – and it means that even should Lord Barlington call, he would not find me at home. That is not what I presume he expects."

Lady Thurston nodded. "I think that he was rather surprised to see that you have friends and acquaintances here. I watched his eyes as we all came in and spoke to you at length. He appeared rather stunned, truth be told! No doubt he believes that he has come to rescue you from some lonely situation when, in fact, that is entirely the opposite."

Temperance smiled and looked out of the window. "That is very true, and I am very grateful for it." As they made their way into the village, Temperance strained to see the carriage in front. A sudden fear licked up her spine. "What if the carriage ahead of us is Lord Barlington?"

Lady Thurston shrugged. "Then we will not get out of the carriage. We will continue to ride around the village and out of it again if we must. I will not force you to be in any sort of situation with Lord Barlington. He is the very gentleman we are trying to avoid!"

Temperance smiled, relieved.

"I think that is Lord Calverton's carriage," Lady Thurston continued, her smile lifting. "Though that does appear to be Lord Calverton and my own husband standing to the right hand side there! I knew they were both gone for a ride but I did not think that they were coming to the village!"

Temperance's heart lifted as she heard Lord Calverton's name on her friend's lips. That gentleman had certainly proved himself to *be* a gentleman and she was very grateful indeed to him for his kindness and consideration of her.

"That must be his mother there, then," Lady Thurston continued. "In the carriage, I mean."

"I wonder where she is going." Temperance smiled as her friend waved to her husband from the carriage window, only for the carriage to slow so they might both step out. Temperance drew in deep breath as she saw Lord Calverton smiling at her, aware that she was beginning to find herself drawn to him in a way she had never expected. There was only a friendship between them, of course, for she dared not let herself think of anything else, but all the same, how quickly a friendship had sprung up between them!

"Good afternoon, Lady Temperance!" Lord Thurston bowed and smiled. "I quite forgot that you and my wife were to take the carriage this afternoon."

"We are to go to the haberdashery," Temperance answered, seeing the flicker of interest in Lord Calverton's eyes as she spoke. "There are some buttons, ribbon and lace that Lady Thurston has been seeking and I myself hope to find that a parcel has been delivered there for me."

"For your artwork?"

She nodded in answer to Lord Thurston's question.

"Then you will be in fine company, for my mother is also hoping for such a thing!" Lord Calverton beamed and then gestured to the other carriage, which had stopped a little ways ahead of them. "I believe she has ordered a good many things so mayhap you will both find yourselves contented!"

Temperance smiled and then waved to Lady Calverton, who stepped down from the carriage with a broad smile on her face. Without hesitating, Temperance made her way to join her and, after a few words of greeting, they walked into the haberdashery together.

***

"Alas, it seems that Lady Temperance is to be disappointed."

Temperance quickly shook her head and tried to smile, hiding her own true feelings of frustration. "I am sure they will come very soon."

"Ah, but not soon enough, I am sure!" Lady Calverton replied, sympathetically. "I understand that you are waiting for these things with great eagerness, for you will want to begin using them right away, will you not?"

From the look in the lady's eyes, Temperance knew that she understood and that, therefore, there was no point in pretending otherwise. "Indeed, that is so. Some of my paintbrushes have become a little weak and I was hoping that I would receive the new ones I ordered so that I might continue painting. I was also looking for a few new paints and the like but… " With a sigh, she lifted her shoulders and then let them fall. "I can be a little more patient, I am sure."

"Could you not come to look at all the many things *I* have?" Lady Calverton's expression lit up. "I would be very glad indeed to share them with you and indeed, since I have just received my shipment, I would be thrilled to let you use whatever you might wish to take."

Temperance quickly shook her head. "I could not."

"But what if I insist!"

A hand went to Temperance's back, making her start in surprise, only for Lord Calverton to lean close to her. He was smiling, his eyes on his mother but she barely heard a word he said, such was her overwhelming awareness of his closeness.

"My mother is most insistent, Lady Temperance. I fear you have very little choice but to accept. I have learned myself that it is the easiest way for one to live."

Lady Calverton laughed and swiped the air between her son and herself while Temperance attempted to smile. The difficulty was that her heart was racing, her skin prickling where Lord Calverton's hand rested on her back and her face growing hot. What was this that was happening to her? Lord Calverton was a friend, was he not? Then why was she responding to his closeness in such a way? It was nothing but foolishness, she reminded herself, for what gentleman would look at a scarred lady in such a way? She was reacting to his friendship in a ridiculous manner and ought to get ahold of herself.

"You *will* come, will you not?" Lady Calverton put a hand on Temperance's arm and smiled. "Tomorrow?"

"It would pull you away from any potential... unexpected encounters."

Temperance glanced over her shoulder to see Lady Thurston arching an eyebrow, smiling at her. "Yes, I understand what you mean."

"Excellent, then it is settled." Lady Calverton beamed at her. "I shall send the carriage for you. Why do you not join us for dinner?"

"I... I am not certain if... " Aware that her mother and father might be a little frustrated that she was absent at such a time, Temperance considered what her aunt would say and, in doing so, found herself smiling. "Yes, I should be glad to. That is very kind of you, Lady Calverton."

"Not at all! It is a delight to me that you will join us. I have been very eager to talk with you about my art, as you well know. It seems now that you will not be able to escape them!" With a smile, Lady Calverton turned away, leaving Temperance to stand alone with Lord Calverton, for Lady Thurston had made her way across the shop also. A little uncertain as to what to say, she looked up at him and then pulled her gaze away, wondering at the sudden sharpness in his gaze.

"There is something I must speak to you about, Lady Temperance."

A knot came into her throat and she nodded, though she did not say anything.

"It is as regards Lord Barlington."

Her eyes flared. "Oh?" For a moment, she feared that he might tell her that he now thought it best for her to return to that gentleman's arms, only for that thought to fly quickly away. Of course it would not be such a thing!

"Lord Thurston and I saw him in the tavern this afternoon. Whether or not he is still there, I could not say. However," the gentleman continued, "both Lord Thurston and I have decided that we will do what we can to make certain of Lord Barlington's presence here. That means that we will appear to be striking up a friendship with him but, in truth, it will only be to make certain as to his intentions and as to where he might be considering going – and what he is thinking about doing!"

A little confused, Temperance frowned. "What do you mean?"

"I mean that if he tells us – because we are better acquainted – that he intends to call upon you tomorrow afternoon, then we will be able to tell you in advance of such an intention."

"And I will be able to step away," Temperance murmured, understanding at once and finding herself all the more grateful for such a suggestion. "That is very kind of you both."

Lord Calverton shook his head. "No, not in the least. As Lord Thurston himself said, you are a dear friend to his wife and to himself and while we have only just become acquainted, I find myself eager to protect you where I can. This situation is dreadful and I am sorry that you have been set to it."

Temperance smiled and then, reaching out one hand, pressed his for a moment. It was only the briefest of moments, the smallest of touches and yet she found herself overwhelmed by it. "My thanks both to you and to Lord Thurston for such consideration," she managed to say, her emotions swimming through her. "You are very kind and most gracious."

Lord Calverton smiled as she released his hand. "We seek only to do you good, Lady Temperance. You have friends here, friends who will do all they can to help you. I only wanted to warn you of this so that when you see me present with Lord Barlington, when you see me acquainting myself with him, you will not be upset and confused."

"Again, I thank you for your consideration," Temperance answered, her hands clasping at her heart. "You are quite right, I would have thought the very worst and might have become very confused indeed."

"I would not want that." Lord Calverton's expression grew fervent. "I want you to think well of me, Lady Temperance."

She smiled at him, seeing the searching way he looked at her, his usual serious expression etched across his face. "You need have no concern in that regard, Lord Calverton. I already do."

***

"And these are the new paintbrushes which arrived yesterday. Please, if any of them are what you are looking for, then I insist that you take them."

Temperance smiled and reached out to touch the paintbrushes, picking up one with a small, thin tip. "I would tell you that I cannot do such a thing, that I *would* not do such a thing but I fear that you would ignore my request and then insist that I do so."

Lady Calverton laughed softly. "I think that you are quite right," she agreed. "I confess that I can be most insistent. It is a trait that my son does not particularly appreciate but I have always found myself to be rather determined." She gestured to the paintbrush. "Now, if this is the paintbrush that you desire, then please do take it. I can have another one sent."

Temperance took it with a nod of thanks. "I want to do some fine detail on some of my recent work," she explained, seeing the interest flood Lady Calverton's expression. "I paint the landscape around my aunt's manor but the detail can sometimes be lacking. I wish very much to improve upon that."

"I see." Lady Calverton tilted her head. "I would be delighted to see some of your work, Lady Temperance. I understand that you may be reluctant to share it with me but – "

Temperance held up one hand, palm out. "Please, do not think that I am reluctant any longer. I have, in fact, brought some pieces with me. They are still in the carriage but I thought I might bring them in to show you, if that would be agreeable?"

Lady Calverton gasped, her eyes wide with a sudden joy. "Of course it would be! I have heard so much about your work from your aunt and I am certain that she has not spoken out of turn about them!

Temperance laughed. "Family are inclined towards boastfulness when it comes to such things, are they not?"

"Mayhap they are but on this occasion, I am sure your aunt does not exaggerate."

Smiling, Temperance thanked Lady Calverton again for the paintbrush. There was some discussion over the new paints as well and Temperance found herself clutching not only the paintbrush but also a few new paints.

"Now, let me have the footman take those to the carriage for you — and mayhap they might bring your paintings to the drawing room?" The slight gleam in Lady Calverton's eye made Temperance flush, praying that the lady would not be disappointed in what she saw.

"Very well." Taking in a deep breath, Temperance tried to fill her heart with courage as Lady Calverton quickly instructed the footman on what to do. Just as the footman returned, however, a cloth-covered bundle in his hands, the door opened to reveal none other than Lord Calverton.

Temperance's heart dropped. She had not thought that she would be showing her work to Lord Calverton! How relieved she was that she had not brought her painting of him standing on the shore.

"Good afternoon." Lord Calverton smiled, bowed and then looked to his mother. "I hope you are well?"

"I am, I thank you."

Lord Calverton looked to Temperance. "And you also?"

She nodded, her heart beating a little more quickly as he looked with interest to the bundle which the footman still held.

"Lady Temperance is just about to show me some of her work," Lady Calverton explained, as her son's eyebrows lifted. "We have had an excellent conversation about such things and you cannot know how thrilled I am that she has been confident enough to bring us some of her paintings!"

Temperance looked from Lady Calverton to Lady Calverton and then to the paintings which the footman held. Lord Calverton was not about to step away, it seemed, and she could not ask him to do so. It would be very rude indeed given that this was his house. There was nothing for her to do but begin to show her work, even with his unexpected presence.

"Please, Lady Temperance." Lady Calverton gestured to the paintings and with a breath, Temperance nodded and went to take them from the footman. Her hands trembled as she set them on the nearby table and unwrapped the cloth, setting out the first and then the second.

When she got to the third, however, Temperance trembled violently. What had she done? This was the very painting she had thought important to leave at home! And yet, somehow, she had chosen and wrapped the very painting she had wanted to hide. She glanced to where Lord Calverton and his mother stood quietly, talking to each other and waiting for her to finish setting her paintings out. What was she to do? She could not pretend that she did not have a third one, could not leave it wrapped up in cloths. They would wonder why she had not done so and there might be a suggestion that she had forgotten it! Her face grew hot as she picked it up, aware that she had no other choice but to set it out.

Then, she turned to Lord Calverton and his mother, gesturing to her paintings but struggling to look at either of them in the face. "Please."

Lady Calverton let out a quiet squeal, though she did not rush forward. Instead, she came near Temperance and put one hand on her arm, smiling back at her. "I know how difficult this is for you," she said, softly. "Thank you for trusting me with this, Lady Temperance. I can already see just how wonderful your work is."

Temperance smiled back, her nervousness abating just a little. "Thank you. Please."

With a nod, Lady Calverton stepped away and Temperance turned, her hands clasped together and at her mouth as she watched Lady Calverton go to the first painting. Her son soon joined her and the murmurs they shared sounded rather positive, which Temperance was relieved about. The closer they came to the third painting, however, the more her anxiety grew. Would either of them realize that she had drawn Lord Calverton as the man standing on the shore? Or would they think that it was simply a figure which she had plucked from her imagination?

As they stood at the third painting, Temperance closed her eyes so as to shut out the sight. She let out a slow breath, her hands tightening, only to hear Lady Calverton let out an exclamation.

Her eyes flew open.

"This is the most wonderful piece I have ever seen, Lady Temperance!"

Temperance blinked furiously.

"It is truly magnificent! I can see the sea, the light settling on the waves and the storm clouds above it. And then there is this solitary figure, standing on the shore and looking out towards it, defiant, determined and without fear." She shook her head, then turned her back on Temperance so that she might look at the painting again. "It is a very strong painting, Lady Temperance. You have made this the most extraordinary painting, where I can almost *feel* the wind whipping through my hair and feel the rain on my cheeks. And yet, there is this one gentleman, standing steady and facing it without concern." She let out a slow breath, then looked back over her shoulder at Temperance. "It is wonderful."

"You may keep it, if you wish."

The words came from Temperance before she could stop them, her face flaming with heat as Lady Calverton's eyes flew wide.

"Are you certain?"

What can I do but consent?

"But of course," she smiled, her heart pounding furiously as Lord Calverton turned to look at her. "If you are truly so taken with it, then – "

"Oh, I am not at all pretending!" Lady Calverton exclaimed, hurrying towards her and grasping Temperance's hands. "This means a great deal to me, Lady Temperance. You cannot know how much I admire your work! Your paintings are exquisite, the detail in them so beautiful! Truly, I am in awe of you."

Temperance blushed but smiled her thanks, having very little certainty as to what it was she could say. Lady Calverton's effusiveness certainly appeared to be genuine, though Temperance's eyes continued to pull towards Lord Calverton. What was it *he* thought of her work?

"I am overwhelmed, truly." Lady Calverton released Temperance's hands and then turned back to the painting, leaving Temperance to stand close to Lord Calverton.

She swallowed, hard.

"You are remarkable, Lady Temperance."

Her chest tightened as Lord Calverton looked over his shoulder to the paintings, then back towards her. His hazel eyes seemed more green than brown and the serious expression on his face was lifted suddenly as he smiled.

"I mean every word, for I can see the doubt in your eyes," Lord Calverton continued, with a small flicker in his own eyes. "Thank you for sharing your work with us, and especially for giving the painting to my mother. It means a great deal to her."

"I am only glad that she likes it so much."

Lord Calverton reached out, took her hand and bent over it. "You are an incredible young lady, Temperance. I should not be surprised at your generosity, for it is yet another example of your sweet nature. I think that all of your paintings are quite remarkable, but the one you have done there, the one which my mother loves so much, has captured my attention just as much as it has hers. It is as though you have captured a single moment – a moment which both myself and others will know so well."

Temperance swallowed and hoped that the tightness in her throat would not make her voice rasp. "What moment, might I ask?"

"Why, the moment where you are standing alone on the shore, feeling the wind around you, seeing the waves before you and wondering why you feel such a calmness within yourself," came the reply, as tears suddenly came to Temperance's eyes. "There has always been something about this place, something about the shore which has called to my heart. As a boy and as a young man, I have stood there many a time and even now, upon my return, I have done the very same."

"You understand my work," Temperance whispered, her fingers tightening on his for a moment. "You see what I have been trying to convey."

His smile sent warmth spiraling up into his eyes. "Who could not?"

Temperance winced inwardly, recalling how her mother had marched into the parlor only yesterday, had looked at her work but had made some vague, banal comment about it. "Not everyone has that same understanding, Lord Calverton. I am very glad indeed that you and your mother see it in that way."

Lord Calverton's smile lingered, his expression softening as he released her hand. "Remarkable," he murmured, as heat curled in Temperance's stomach. "Truly remarkable."

"I quite agree." Lady Calverton came back towards them and the moment Temperance and Lord Calverton had shared faded away. "Thank you again, Lady Temperance. You cannot know how much your gift has touched my heart."

Temperance put one hand to her heart and inclined her head.

"And now, to dinner, where we shall talk more about artistic things and watch as my son attempts to remain engaged but struggles to do so," Lady Calverton laughed, making Temperance laugh. "I am thrilled to have you here with us, Lady Temperance. I hope this will be the beginning of a great many number of conversations."

Temperance nodded. "Yes, Lady Calverton. I am certain it shall be."

Chapter Sixteen

"There he is."

James nodded in Lord Barlington's direction, just as Lord Thurston turned his head to see.

"Ah, yes. I see him."

"He is talking to Lady Temperance."

Lord Thurston glanced at him. "Yes, but I believe given that we are all down at the shore, he is permitted to speak to whomever he wishes. Though her aunt is with her, so I do not think that you need to be too concerned."

James scowled but said nothing. He and Lord Thurston had taken a walk to the shore and upon approaching the top of the cliffs, had spied the very gentleman they had been speaking off hurrying down the path. James had very little doubt that he had been informed – no doubt by Lady Temperance's parents – that this was where she was to be found.

"It seems that he will not be stopped," Lord Thurston murmured, as both James and himself continued to make their way down the path to the shore, though it took all of James' restraint not to rush down and then hurry towards Lady Temperance. "You did speak to the lady about the situation, did you not?"

James nodded.

"And she is in agreement?"

"Yes, she is. It was a wise suggestion for me to go to speak to her about what was happening. She did understand and was grateful to both of us for what we are attempting to do."

Lord Thurston glanced at him. "That is good."

"And now we must pretend to be delighted with his company," James muttered, rubbing one hand over his eyes. "I do not want to even *look* at the fellow and yet now I must pretend as though I am glad to be speaking with him again."

His friend chuckled. "We can do this. You shall have to remove that seriousness from your expression, however, and attempt to look more jovial!"

There was no time for James to reply for by the time they had reached Lady Temperance, Lady Hartford and Lord Barlington, all three turned to face them at once. The relief which flickered in Lady Temperance's eyes was unmistakable.

"Good afternoon, Lord Calverton, Lord Thurston!" Lord Barlington's enthusiasm made James frown, though he hid this with a bow instead.

"Good afternoon to you all." James looked to Lady Temperance and offered her a smile. "It is not a bad afternoon for a walk by the shore, though a little windy."

"Which is why I am eagerly discussing my plans for a ball!" Lord Barlington exclaimed, looking back at Lady Temperance as though he wanted to grasp her attention over James. "A ball! What say you to that, then? It would be marvelous, would it not? I think I shall have it in a sennight, for – "

"Not in a sennight, no." Lord Thurston chortled and Lord Barlington immediately frowned. "You cannot do such a thing in a sennight. This is not London! You will have to send for a good many things and it will take many days before they arrive."

"Oh. I had not thought of such a thing." Lord Barlington rubbed one hand over his chin and looked away. "A fortnight then? Mayhap three weeks?" His eyes went back to Lady Temperance. "And what would you say to that, Lady Temperance? Might I hope that you would be agreeable to such a thing?"

Lady Temperance was not looking directly at Lord Barlington, James noticed. Instead, her eyes were somewhere around his shoulder.

"I am not certain if a ball would be a good occasion to have here," she said, crisply. "There are not that many gentry and – "

"I am sure that everyone will come if they are invited!" Lord Barlington interrupted, making James frown and Lady Temperance roll her eyes – albeit without the gentleman seeing her. "No-one else has thrown a ball here as yet, I have discovered, so there is no reason that they should not have one now. There are more gentry here than you might think, Lady Temperance, though not all of them fine or high society. I think it is an excellent idea and I fully intend to pursue it." He looked again to Lady Temperance and the glint in his eye made James frown, hard. Without hesitating, he looked to Lady Temperance himself.

"If this ball goes as Lord Barlington plans, might you be willing to attend with me, Lady Temperance?"

Lord Barlington cleared his throat, his brows furrowing. "Forgive me, Lord Calverton, but I – "

"How very kind of you, Lord Calverton. Of course, I should be glad to accept." There came a flash of relief into Lady Temperance's eyes, followed by a quick smile. Lord Barlington, on the other hand, frowned hard.

"You are aware the invitations have not gone out as yet," he muttered, making James' eyebrows lift. Would this gentleman truly refuse to invite him to this ball?

"Well, I am certain that you will want as many gentry as possible at the ball," Lord Thurston interjected, an easy smile on his lips though James caught the steel in his friend's eyes. "Though you should be careful with what you say, Lord Barlington. Invitations might not have been given out as yet, but neither, therefore, have there been any acceptances. It could be that those you presumed would accept might find themselves unfortunately already occupied on that evening."

James shot his friend a small smile, though Lord Thurston did not so much as glance at him. Lord Barlington, after a moment, let out a small, choked laugh and then shook his head.

"And now I know that you must be jesting," he stated, waggling one finger at Lord Thurston. "Just as I am, of course. Everyone here shall receive an invitation!"

"Good." Lord Thurston clicked his heels smartly, then smiled and stepped forward. "My dear wife will be most displeased that she chose to remain at home, given that we have found you here. Should you like to take a short walk along the shoreline with me?"

Lady Temperance nodded. "Yes, of course, Lord Thurston." She offered them all a small smile. "Do excuse me."

Seeing what it was that Lord Thurston had done in taking Lady Temperance away, James looked back to Lord Barlington. Grateful that Lady Hartford was still present but knowing that he was to do something to make Lord Barlington feel as though James was interested in his company, James forced a smile.

"I should be very interested to hear if you have made any recent improvements to your estate, Lord Barlington?" he began, not knowing one thing about the gentleman's situation. "I did hear the Duke of Danfield state that you have the very finest of homes."

Lord Barlington looked back at him for a moment before he began, as though he were wondering whether or not James spoke the truth or if this was some ploy or other. It did not take long, however, for Lord Barlington to begin to speak about his estate and, with that, to go into great detail about the many fine things about it. James forced that smile to linger on his face even though he did not have any real interest in what was being said. He nodded and murmured and did all the things which made it sound as though he were truly intrigued while, inwardly, felt his heart twisting with frustration. This gentleman seemed to think that he was somehow the very greatest of fellows in all of England! He spoke highly of everything he owned, everything he did and everything that brought him pleasure, and did not once ask either James or Lady Hartford anything about their own situations.

"How very interesting," Lady Hartford murmured, casting a quick look towards James who returned her look with a small, slightly wry smile. "You seem to have been very fortunate in a good many things, Lord Barlington."

"Ah yes, very fortunate indeed." Lord Barlington sighed, smiled and then looked to where Lady Temperance and Lord Thurston were walking. James followed his eyes and found himself scowling. How dare this gentleman look to Lady Temperance in such a way? *He* had been the one to remove himself from her, *he* had been the one who had told her that they could no longer wed. Why, now, was he gazing at her with such longing? He had caused her so much difficulty, pain and sorrow and now *he* was the one seeking her out?

"I think that it may well be time to take our leave." Lady Hartford threw a smile to Lord Barlington, then turned to James. "Might you be willing to walk with me, Lord Calverton? I do find the sand a little hard to walk in at some points." She looked to Lord Barlington. "Good afternoon, Lord Barlington."

"Good afternoon." Lord Barlington bowed, making as though he wished to say something more, only for James to step forward, taking Lady Hartford's arm and begin to walk away. He threw a quick farewell over his shoulder and then continued on his way towards Lord Thurston and Lady Temperance, filled with relief when Lord Barlington did not follow.

"You are very good to keep Lord Barlington talking so that my dear niece does not have to be near him," Lady Hartford murmured, as they walked across the sand. "I think she was already struggling with his presence when you joined us and hearing him speak about this ball... well, if you had not asked her if she would accompany you, then I do not know what we would have done!"

"That is quite all right." James offered Lady Hartford a small smile, then shook his head. "Lord Barlington's intentions are something I do not understand. Why he must pursue Lady Temperance when she is the one who has been so severely injured by him, I cannot tell."

"Nor can I," Lady Hartford sighed. "But one way or another, I am certain that Lord Barlington will make himself clear... and to the detriment of Lady Temperance."

James scowled. "I will do my level best to do whatever I can to help that," he said, earning himself another grateful smile from the lady. "And if there is to be a ball, then I certainly shall take Lady Temperance along with me and protect her from him in any way I can." He looked to Lady Hartford, taking in her small smile. "I will promise you that."

Chapter Seventeen

"Temperance?"

Turning, Temperance looked at the door, expecting to see her aunt standing in the doorway. Instead, she saw her mother as she came further into the room. Temperance swallowed hard, her joy evaporating. She had spent a very pleasant few hours painting and, much to her own surprise, had found herself painting something rather different from her usual efforts. Instead of painting a seascape, instead of looking at the waves and the swirling clouds above it, she had begun to paint a gentleman and a lady, walking arm in arm along the shore. She had been reminded of the happiness which had filled her heart when she had seen Lord Calverton and her aunt walking arm in arm towards her on the beach. They had been smiling and laughing at each other as though they had been friends for a very long time – and after that, her happiness had increased as she had watched Lord Barlington take his leave.

She had a great and a tremendous fear that her mother was about to speak of Lord Barlington all over again.

"You are doing a great deal of painting, Temperance." Her mother clicked her tongue and shook her head. "I think it is a little *too* much, frankly."

"I enjoy painting, Mama," she replied, not letting her mother's words cut at her heart too much. "It brings me a great deal of joy."

"Then you must find other things that bring you joy," came the reply, as though this was something that Temperance was doing wrong. "In speaking of that, Temperance, I think it is high time that you listened to all that Lord Barlington wishes to say to you."

Temperance immediately shook her head. "No. I have no desire to speak to him about anything at all."

"Be that as it may, your father and I have discussed this and we have both decided that it would be right for you to do so. Whether you would be glad to hear him or not, it is only polite for you to hear what he has to say. After all, Temperance, he has given up a great deal for you!"

"Given up a great deal?" Temperance repeated, her voice rising a little with anger. "What is it that he has 'given up' for me?"

Her mother planted her hands at her hips. "Temperance, you are being unreasonable! He has given up the London Season in order to be here near you! He has set aside all that he could gain from that and has, instead, come to seek you out."

"And I do not want to see him," Temperance stated, firmly, flinging up one hand towards her face. "Do you not see this? Do you not recall how he treated me thereafter?"

"I do not think that you can judge him harshly at all!" her mother exclaimed. "He came and spoke to you, did he not? He eagerly requested a conversation with you and it is *you* who has refused him."

Temperance shook her head and said nothing more, turning back to her painting though she did not truly see it. Her vision blurred as she blinked back hot tears, wishing that her mother could show her even the smallest semblance of understanding.

"Now, he will be here in a few minutes and I expect you to listen to everything that he has to say."

Twisting around, Temperance stared at her mother, though the Duchess lifted her chin and gazed back at her without a word, almost daring her to challenge what she had said.

"I... I cannot, I – "

"You will tolerate him for a few minutes, Temperance." The Duchess sniffed and then turned on her heel. "And do not think that you can take your leave. I will be standing directly outside, waiting for him to arrive. Thereafter, I will stand at the open door and allow him to speak freely. Do you understand?"

Temperance swallowed at the tightness in her throat, trying desperately to find something to say, her heart pounding furiously but from the look in her mother's eyes, she realized it wouldn't make any difference. Her mother had determined what she was to do and that was all there was to it. The Duchess stepped out of the room, the door closed and Temperance stared at it for some moments, her whole body suddenly growing cold.

What can I do?

Hurriedly, she grasped some paper and, after a few moments, composed two short notes. Ringing the bell, Temperance paced back and forth, waiting for the maid.

"Temperance?" Her mother lifted an eyebrow as the maid came in behind her. "What is the meaning of this? You are not going to use the maid to escape!"

"I was only going to request a tea tray, Mama, and a bowl to wash my hands before Lord Barlington arrives," Temperance answered, her voice trembling furiously as she beckoned the maid closer. "And there are some things here which need to be removed."

Her mother lifted an eyebrow but said nothing, giving only a brief nod and then making her way back to the door.

"Have this sent to Lord Calverton at once," Temperance murmured, handing the first note to the maid. "And this to Lady Thurston. At once, you understand?"

The maid nodded. "What else am I to do here, my lady?"

Temperance shook her head. "Nothing. Now go with all haste." As the maid left, Temperance drew in a deep breath and then set her shoulders. Lord Barlington was going to come into her private parlor, a place where she had found herself a little healed from the pain he had caused her, and would, instead, shatter the peace which she now held so dear.

But what could she do? Her mother had basically confined her to this room, determining that she *would* hear all that Lord Barlington had to say, no matter what she herself wanted!

Her eyes closed as she trembled visibly, her anxiety increasing every moment that she waited for his arrival. This had all been arranged without her consent and now all she could do was wait.

***

"Finally, we are to be able to speak, face to face and without interruption."

Temperance did not go to sit down as Lord Barlington came into the room. Instead, keeping her chin lifted – despite the trembling in her frame – she stepped behind the couch and set her hands to it, her fingers curling into the soft fabric.

"I am grateful for the time you are willing to give me," Lord Barlington continued, coming to stand a little closer to her, though he stayed enough of a distance away to leave Temperance a little more at ease. "There is so much that I wish to say. I think that – "

"It is my mother who has determined that I am to speak with you," Temperance interjected, not at all concerned that she had interrupted him so quickly. "I did not know of this arrangement. I was not told of it."

Lord Barlington, rather than appearing at all concerned by this, rather than stating that he was sorry such a thing had happened, merely shrugged and Temperance's stomach twisted. To her mind, it was clear just how little Lord Barlington cared for her, even if he pretended to be doing so.

"I am grateful for the opportunity to say all that I wish to say," he said, taking a few steps closer to the couch, though Temperance silently vowed to keep a piece of furniture between them no matter how much he tried to do otherwise. "Lady Temperance, you must know how much I regret what I did."

"Your regret does not matter to me."

"Though it should!" came the reply. "It could change a great deal between us if only you would consider what I have to say."

Temperance shook her head. "No, Lord Barlington. Nothing will change between us."

"But I am *truly* sorry," he said, his tone beseeching, his eyes a little wide as though by his words and his expression, he might convince her. "I should never have turned from you. The scar is severe, yes, but that does not mean that *you* have altered!"

"And yet, you broke our engagement because of it!" Temperance exclaimed, a deep anger beginning to push its way through her, anger which had remained unspoken for the last two years. "You told me that I was worth nothing to you any longer, that this *imperfection* was not something you could endure, as though *you* were the one suffering. You did not have any real concern for me; you only thought of yourself. And now you come to me, expecting me to be grateful for your return and your apology?"

"Perhaps not grateful," Lord Barlington murmured, his voice soft but a glint in his eye which Temperance did not like. "Though I did hope that you would understand."

Temperance shook her head, silently praying that Lord Barlington would either quit the room or that Lord Calverton or Lady Thurston would appear and be able to bring her the relief she so desperately craved.

"I want to try again, Temperance." Lord Barlington moved to make his way around the couch towards her but Temperance moved quickly, keeping the piece of furniture between them. "Why do you avoid me so? Why do you hurry away? Can you not see that this connection, this *closeness* is something that would be good for the two of us?"

"No, it would not be," she answered, her voice rasping a little as fear began to climb up her throat. What if Lord Barlington attempted to force himself into a situation where they might be then 'discovered' by her mother, thereby forcing a connection between them again? He was not a good, kind-hearted, understanding gentleman and his clear expectation that she would accept him might very well force him to act in such a desperate manner. What if she could not escape him?

"You are mistaken if you think that lingering here, in this house as a spinster, will be any better for you," Lord Barlington continued, his lip curling just a little. "Come now, Temperance, do be reasonable. Can you not see how devoted I am to you? I have given up society life, I have made arrangements to reside near you, all so that I might express just how eager I am for us to return to what we once shared."

Temperance's breath came quick and fast as she continued to move slowly, keeping a distance between Lord Barlington and herself. "You think that you have all the answers to my present difficulties, Lord Barlington, but you presume too much. You believe I am upset, that I am sorrowful in where I am at present when I assure you, I am quite the opposite. I do not require you to come back to rescue me. I do not require you to pull me from spinsterhood."

Lord Barlington clicked his tongue. "Yes, you do. You merely do not see it as yet."

The arrogance with which he spoke made her both angry and stunned that he should think it quite suitable for him to speak to her in such a manner. Did he truly believe that he had the right to tell her such things? That he was some how required to give her such advice?

"I made a mistake, Temperance," he said, firmly. "I want now to rectify it."

"That is *your* desire," she answered, attempting to speak with as much firmness as he. "It is not mine and you cannot force that upon me."

Something passed over Lord Barlington's expression which gripped Temperance's heart with a terror she could not explain. Lord Barlington's jaw tightened, his eyes narrowed and fixed to hers. There was a hint of steel in them, a slight narrowing of the edges of his eyes that made Temperance's heart squeeze with fright. She looked to the door, wondering if her mother was suddenly going to burst into the room in the hope that something untoward was taking place.

"Come now, Temperance, do be reasonable." There was a darkness to Lord Barlington's tone which made her shudder violently. "I have never stopped caring for you. These last two years have been torment, separated from you in a way which has torn at my heart. To realize that the sadness and upset upon me were my own doing made my guilt and embarrassment grow to such heights, they could not be tolerated! It was then that I decided to do what I had to in order to try and bring about a healing between us."

Temperance did not believe a single word which came from his mouth. There was no genuine emotion there, no hint of promise in anything that he had to say. Temperance tried to think of an answer, tried to find a way to tell him that nothing that he said to her, nothing that he expressed, would make any difference to her heart but, in the end, chose to say nothing. To her mind, it seemed that anything she tried to say would either be rejected or turned back on her, as though somehow *she* were the one in the wrong for refusing to accept him.

"I beg of you to consider all I have said, Temperance." Lord Barlington made his way towards her again but quickly, she stepped behind the couch once more. Instantly, the darkness on Lord Barlington's expression grew heavier.

"Temperance," he said, in a somewhat commanding tone, "you are being foolish. There is no need for these games! I – "

"Ah, here you are! I should have known you would be painting."

Relief poured into Temperance's veins and, feeling suddenly weak, she made her way around and sat down heavily on the couch, just as Lord Calverton came a little further into the room.

His smile was broad but the way his eyes sparkled with obvious concern made Temperance aware of just how much he was worried.

"My mother insisted that we come to call for she has just found the most wonderful scene and wishes to speak to you about it," Lord Calverton continued, giving Lord Barlington a brief nod. "You know very well what my mother is like, I am afraid!"

"Yes, I do." Temperance managed a faint smile, her heartbeat finally slowing, only for Lady Thurston to come sailing into the room.

"And here I am at last, Temperance," she said, ignoring Lord Barlington completely. "I know you were expecting me to call a little earlier, but I confess that I took a little too long to choose my bonnet. Now," she continued, smiling warmly as she sat down beside Temperance, "should you like to show me your most recent painting? Or are we to wait for Lady Calverton?"

Temperance managed another smile. "Lord Calverton has just told me that his mother is eager to speak with me so yes, I think we should wait for her to arrive."

"She will be here presently. I took my horse and she was having the carriage prepared by the time I left." Lord Calverton smiled at her and then sat down, making his presence felt in the room. It was not as though he was going to be taking his leave at any time and from the way Lord Barlington frowned, Temperance was sure that he was more than a little frustrated at the interruption.

"Then I will have the tea trays brought here," Temperance murmured, as Lady Thurston reached to press her hand for a moment, her action making Temperance's courage rise all the more. "Thank you both for coming." She smiled, not looking to Lord Barlington. "I am sure we will have a very pleasant afternoon indeed."

Chapter Eighteen

James sat back in his chair and let out a long, contented breath. He had enjoyed an excellent morning, with a walk along the top of the cliffs and, thereafter, had sat down to do a little correspondence. He had received some excellent news from his solicitors, informing him that his investments were doing very well indeed, and his estate manager had also written with the news that the crops were doing well and the tenants all quite contented. After a quiet luncheon, he was now stretched out on the bench by the gardens, enjoying the afternoon sunshine. It was a sheltered spot, hiding him from the wind which seemed to be ever-present, and James found his entire body softening as he relaxed. It was warm and he was contented, his thoughts drifting towards Lady Temperance as he lay in the sunshine.

I do care for her.

James let a smile drift across his face as he recalled how he had asked Lady Temperance to the ball. She had been thrilled, glad that he had saved her from Lord Barlington and though James himself was pleased that he had been of assistance to her, he was also well aware that his own heart had filled with a pleasure he had not yet been able to remove from himself. He did not *want* it gone either, all too aware that his consideration of Lady Temperance was growing steadily. The scar on her cheek was not something that he ever even thought of, never even considered. Instead, he thought of her beauty of character, the sweetness of her nature, of her beautiful emerald eyes, the tenderness of her smile and the golden tresses which framed her face. To his mind, Lady Temperance was one of the most remarkable young ladies he had ever had the chance to meet – and that only added to the affection he felt towards her.

Affection which might soon lead to something a little more profound.

That thought did not frighten him, as he might have once suspected. Instead, he found himself smiling, his eyes still closed as he considered what might soon be waiting for him in his future.

His smile faded.

Though she did say how contented she was as a spinster. What if I am to be rejected? What if all that she expresses to me is nothing more than a gratitude for what I am doing to prevent Lord Barlington from pursuing her?

That was something James had to consider. It could be that, despite his own tender heart, Lady Temperance might not feel the same way as he did. What then? Would his confession of affection – should he make it – set them both apart, breaking the connection they had built thus far? Would he risk that in the hope that he might gain something more?

Someone coughed lightly and James opened his eyes, squinting up as he shaded his eyes with his hand. "Yes?"

"You have received an urgent note from Lady Temperance, my lord."

In an instant, James sat up and practically snatched the note from the butler's hand. Opening it, he read the few lines and then, after a moment, got to his feet.

"Have my horse prepared immediately and with the greatest haste," he told the butler, already making his way back towards the house. "Where is my mother? I must speak with her."

"She is painting, my lord."

James broke into a run, rushing back inside and making his way directly to the drawing room. He could hear his mother humming as he drew near, though he did not apologise for the interruption.

"Mother, I must take my leave at once. Might you come with me? Lady Temperance has sent an urgent note. It seems as though Lord Barlington has been invited to speak with her – I presume her mother or father has done so – though she herself has no desire to speak with him. She is in her parlor and might be left quite alone!"

His mother's eyes flared. "You mean to say that she would be left alone with Lord Barlington?"

James nodded. "Yes. My horse is being prepared as we speak. Will you take the carriage? Make some excuse as to why you must go to see her?"

Clearly understanding the concern, Lady Calverton set down her brush. "Of course. Goodness, whatever is the Duchess thinking? I thought Temperance had made it plain that she does not want to be closer acquainted with Lord Barlington and yet – "

"I must go, Mother!" James exclaimed, rushing back to the door. "She has asked me for help and I cannot delay!"

Within a few minutes, he was astride his horse, riding as fast as he could towards Lady Hartford's manor. He had no doubt that Lady Hartford herself would be entirely unaware of this scheme, would not know that Lady Temperance was to be alone with Lord Barlington, for if she had been present, James was certain she would never have allowed it.

Jumping down from his mount, James took a few moments to steady himself. He was breathing rather quickly, and though he gave his hat and gloves to the butler, he still paused to brush one hand through his hair.

"I have come to call on Lady Temperance," he told the butler, somewhat curtly. "Have no concern about bringing me to her, I know where she will be." As he was about to step inside, the sound of carriage wheels caught his attention and, glancing over his shoulder, he saw with relief that Lady Thurston was also arriving. James did not wait for her arrival, however. Instead, he made his way into the house without further hesitation, striding towards the parlor where he knew Lady Temperance would be painting. He had never been inside the room before, of course, but Lady Hartford had pointed it out to him on one previous occasion.

"Ah, Your Grace." Seeing the Duchess of Danfield standing outside the door – though it was ajar – James bowed quickly and, seeing the surprise etch itself on her face, chose to use that to his advantage. "I have come to see Lady Temperance, to warn her that my mother is soon to be arriving in the hope of discussing a great many things as regards her artwork. I am sure you understand!" He stepped inside at once, ignoring the slight squeak of protest from the Duchess, his heart slamming hard against his chest at the sight which he came to.

Lady Temperance was standing behind a couch, her hands gripping the top of it, her face white. Lord Barlington, however, appeared to be attempting to approach her from one side, his own expression dark though both of them turned to face him the moment he came inside.

"Ah! Here you are. I should have known that you would be painting." He forced a brightness to his voice as he smiled, then bowed towards Lady Temperance, choosing to ignore Lord Barlington's presence, giving him only the very briefest of nods.

"My mother insisted that we come to call for she has just found the most wonderful scene and wishes to speak to you about it. You know very well what my mother is like, I am afraid!"

"Yes, I do." Lady Temperance managed to smile back at him, only for the door behind James to open wide again. James turned to see Lady Thurston reaching out to greet Lady Temperance, going over to the couch so she might join her there.

"And here I am at last, Temperance," she cried. "I know you were expecting me to call a little earlier, but I confess that I took a little too long to choose my bonnet. Now, should you like to show me your most recent painting? Or are we to wait for Lady Calverton?"

Lady Temperance managed another smile as James chose to sit down also, leaving only Lord Barlington standing. "Lord Calverton has just told me that his mother is eager to speak with me so yes, I think we should wait for her to arrive."

"She will be here presently. I took my horse and she was having the carriage prepared by the time I left." He leaned back, making it quite clear that he was not about to remove himself any time soon. Lady Temperance's shoulders rounded with obvious relief, Lady Thurston gripping her hand.

"Then I will have the tea trays brought here," she said, softly. "Thank you both for coming. I am sure we will have a very pleasant afternoon indeed." She made to rise to ring the bell, but James quickly caught the way she trembled and instead, got to his feet.

"Permit me, Lady Temperance. I can see that Lady Thurston is eager to speak with you so I would not dare deprive you of her company for even a few moments!"

Lady Temperance smiled and sat back down quickly, with Lady Thurston reaching for her hand again, though this time, she looped her arm through Lady Temperance's as though to make it quite plain to Lord Barlington that she was here to stay.

The door opened again, just as James sat back down from ringing the bell. In came not only his mother but a rather flustered looking Duchess. Lady Calverton was chattering quite rapidly and the Duchess was unable to put in a single word to the lady in response.

James hid a smile, glancing sidelong at Lady Temperance and Lady Thurston.

"Ah, there you are Lady Temperance! I see that my son has come to warn you that I was on my way." She laughed and then looked to the Duchess. "Your daughter is very talented, I must say. You cannot know the joy which seeing her work here brings me. From one artist to another, it fills my heart with happiness."

"Thank you," the Duchess murmured, as Lady Calverton came directly towards Lady Temperance. They quickly fell into conversation and James let his gaze wander across the room, though he did watch Lord Barlington with interest. The gentleman was looking to the Duchess, who, after a moment, shook her head, sighed and turned to quit the room. Lord Barlington shrugged to himself and, thereafter, made his way from the room after the Duchess. The moment he stepped out, Lady Temperance dropped her head and put her face in her hands.

James was beside her in a moment, his mother next to him, Lady Thurston beside her.

"Thank you," Lady Temperance whispered, not lifting her head from her hands, her voice muffled. "I was not sure if my notes would reach you in time or even if anyone would come but – "

"Nothing would have stopped my son, I can assure you of that." With a glance towards him, James' mother smiled gently as Lady Temperance dropped her hands and, thereafter, let out a slow breath. "We are here to support you, Lady Temperance. I am sorry if Lord Barlington distressed you."

Lady Temperance blinked rapidly, though she did not let any tears fall. "He is determined to begin our engagement again."

James' heart lurched.

"He almost insists upon it," she continued, her voice growing hoarse. "I was afraid that he would force a situation between us where my mother might then walk into the room and declare that we *must* marry." Her eyes went to James'. "Thank goodness that you arrived when you did."

"I am only sorry I could not get here more quickly."

She managed a small, quiet smile. "You arrived just when I needed you, Lord Calverton. I thank you."

"Now, since we are here, I should very much like to see what you have been working on," Lady Calverton said, her smile gentle. "Though only if you are willing to do so. I know that I am very eager but I do not want to put you under any undue pressure."

Lady Temperance took in a breath and, after a moment, got to her feet. "No, I should be glad to. It might distract me from what has taken place this afternoon."

"And I will pour the tea," Lady Thurston answered, as James looked to Lady Temperance, wondering what he ought to do. He hesitated, then made to go and sit back down. He had not been invited to look at her paintings and did not want to intrude.

"Should you like to join us, Lord Calverton?"

James turned, seeing Lady Temperance looking at him while a faint hint of color had come into her cheeks, her gaze steady. "If you would be willing, then of course. I would be thoroughly delighted to see any of your work."

She smiled and then gestured to her easel, making her way across the room to where her easel stood. James went with her, his heart lifting a little as he came to join her. All the same, he found himself continually troubled, wondering just what Lady Temperance had endured – and might be forced to endure – by Lord Barlington's demands.

Chapter Nineteen

One week later.

"Temperance, I am most displeased with you."

Temperance blinked in surprise as her mother came into the drawing room, seemingly oblivious to the presence of both Lady Hartford and the Duke himself.

"Displeased?" Temperance asked, uncertain as to why her mother had cause to be angry with her. "I do not see why."

"Because you are attending Lord Barlington's ball with a gentleman who is *not* Lord Barlington!" her mother exclaimed, though the Duke's eyebrows lifted in clear surprise at what she had said. "You should have refused Lord Calverton."

"And why should she have done that?" Lady Hartford asked, before Temperance could say anything. "That is a very strange thing to say, sister. I would have thought that you would have been pleased that your daughter had been asked to the ball."

"Indeed, my dear, I do think you are being a little harsh." The Duke, who had not had cause to say anything thus far and, indeed, over the last week had not said a single word of encouragement as regarded Lord Barlington, lifted his shoulders and then let them fall. "Lord Calverton is just as respectable a gentleman as Lord Barlington. Why would you be disappointed that such a fellow would ask Temperance to the ball?"

"Because he is not a Marquess! Lord *Barlington* is a Marquess and we have always said that we want our daughters to marry the very highest title we could manage."

"But you forget that Lord Barlington is not someone that your daughter is inclined towards," Lady Hartford said, spreading out her hands. "But Lord Calverton clearly is. Whether he is a Marquess or not, surely your daughter's own considerations ought to come first."

The Duchess shook her head. "That is foolishness, sister. You know very well that it is the responsibility of a mother to make certain that their child is given as great a situation as possible, regardless of their own seeming sensibilities." She gestured to her husband. "And you yourself said that you believed it would be good for Temperance to consider Lord Barlington again."

"Yes, but that was before it became clear that Lord Calverton was interested in her company also," the Duke replied, a slight heaviness to his tone which grew all the more apparent as he continued to speak. "You may be determined for Temperance to marry a Marquess but I think that an Earl is just as acceptable."

"Thank you, Father," Temperance murmured, relief filling her as she saw her father smile. "Lord Calverton is much more pleasing to me than Lord Barlington, I confess."

"I quite understand."

"Though I do not and I will continue to encourage you towards Lord Barlington," her mother snapped, her face now flushed with obvious anger. "You are making a mistake there, Temperance. You could be a Marchioness rather than a Countess! I could be the mother of such a person and instead, you seek out the lower titled gentleman simply because you are unwilling to forgive Lord Barlington for one foolish mistake."

Temperance curled her hands tightly as she fought the urge to throw back an equally biting remark about Lord Barlington to her mother. To her mind, Lord Barlington was nothing but odious and she was beginning to despise her mother's clear determination to force them back together. It was not about her happiness, Temperance knew, but rather than her mother desired for all her daughters to be as well married as they could be, regardless of their own feelings. How grateful she was now for her aunt and even for her father, glad that *he* was not pushing her towards Lord Barlington also!

A scratch came to the door. "Lord Calverton has arrived," the butler told her, as the Duchess stamped one foot on the floor in obvious frustration.

"Let us go, Temperance," Lady Hartford smiled, as Temperance got to her feet. "We will see you both at the ball."

Temperance nodded and, ignoring the angry look on her mother's face, made her way to the door. She was *more* than ready to escape this conversation and instead, find herself again in the company of Lord Calverton.

***

"Well, for all that Lord Barlington has not been present in this area for long, he does seem to have thrown an excellent ball."

Temperance grimaced as Lord Calverton shot her a look of surprised. "Loathe though I am to admit it, of course!"

He chuckled then, making her smile. "I confess that I am not at all eager to say such a thing about the fellow either, though this room is magnificently decorated, the food is marvelous and the orchestra are quite proficient!"

"Indeed," Temperance sighed, making Lord Calverton's lips twitch as she fought to hide her own laughter. "I will admit that I did very much want for this evening to be something of a failure, though that does reveal my rather cruel heart, does it not?"

Lord Calverton's smile quickly faded as he shook his head. "No, I would not say that there is any cruelty there, Lady Temperance. After all that has taken place, I quite understand it."

"And you do not think ill of me?"

When he shook his head again, Temperance found herself smiling with relief, glad to know that his opinion of her had not faded by such an admittance. She wondered for a moment, if there had been anything other than the hope of saving her from Lord Barlington that had come with his request to accompany her to the ball. She herself had to admit that she found Lord Calverton's company more than a little wonderful and, if the truth were to be known, she was beginning to find herself rather drawn to him. He was a very handsome fellow, with a softness about his character which, despite his often serious expression, brought with it a tenderness of heart. The way he had sought to protect her, the way he had come to her defense time and again and the urgency with which he had responded to her prompting had made her all the more eager for his company. Dare she let herself think that there might be something of a return of her consideration of him? Dare she believe that there was something more to that?

Temperance took in a deep breath and then released it again, aware that she would soon have to step out of the shadows of the back of the room and out into the company of the other guests.

"Should you like to dance this evening, Lady Temperance?" Lord Calverton's voice was soft, a gentleness there which made her heart quicken. "I can understand that you might wish to hide away for the remainder of the evening, however, and if that is the case, then I will be more than delighted to stand with you. Though," he continued, a smile beginning to pull at the sides of his mouth, "I think that you should step forward in courage, regardless of the fact that Lord Barlington is present."

"And despite the fact that others will gaze at my face and whisper about it?" Temperance murmured, feeling the heat in her face grow all the more as Lord Calverton's smile became sympathetic. "I will not pretend that I am unaware of my scar, Lord Calverton. You have been very good not to mention it, but – "

"There is nothing to say," he interrupted, gently. "That scar does not define you. It does not tell me who you are nor what your character is like. Those are things that I have been able to determine simply by being in your company – and I confess to you that what I see is nothing but beautiful."

Temperance smiled quickly, her heart slamming hard against her ribs, a warmth beginning to flood her core. She did not know where to look, finding herself a little uncertain when she let herself glance in his eyes. Was he speaking as a friend might, seeking only to encourage her? Or was there something more there?

"I am sorry for the times you have been rejected or made to feel as though you are worth nothing because of what you bear upon your cheek," Lord Calverton finished, taking a small step closer to her, his voice only a little louder than a whisper now. "I can assure you, I am not someone who would ever do such a thing. I think very highly of you indeed, Lady Temperance. I think you are the most marvelous creature I have ever had opportunity to meet and I count myself blessed for the time we have spent together thus far."

Temperance lifted her chin, Lord Calverton's words bolstering her courage. "Then I *shall* dance," she stated, taking her dance card from her wrist and offering it to him. "Though it has been some time since I have stepped out and therefore, I am a little concerned that I might make some mistake!"

"Ah, there you are!"

Temperance's hand froze on her dance card as she held it out to Lord Calverton, her stomach twisting hard as Lord Barlington came to join them. He reached for the dance card only for Lord Calverton to quickly take it from Temperance's hand.

"I believe that Lady Temperance was offering her dance card to *me,* Lord Barlington," he said, a little smartly. "You would not be rude enough to snatch it from me, I am sure!"

"Oh, of course not."

"And as Lady Temperance has just stated, she may only wish to dance once or two dances." Lord Calverton quickly wrote his name down on two dances and then handed the card back to Temperance, his gaze steady as he gave her a small nod as though to encourage her to remain steady against the face of Lord Barlington's insistence. "Which, of course, is the lady's prerogative."

"And I have no wish to dance with you, Lord Barlington," Temperance interjected, looking into the face of her once-betrothed and lifting her chin a notch. "I have no interest in even continuing a conversation with you, which I am certain you understand."

"I do not understand in the least!" Lord Barlington exclaimed, his expression growing dark with either confusion or anger. "I have done all that I can to beg for your forgiveness for my foolish actions and yet, you seem determined to hold it against me! You will not even tolerate my presence? How can that be?"

"Because you hurt my heart a great deal, you pained my soul and the consequences of your actions lingered long into my life. Though I have begun to recover from it now, thanks to new acquaintances." Temperance let her gaze drift to Lord Calverton and, seeing his hazel eyes soften, let herself smile. "I look forward to our dances, Lord Calverton."

"As do I." He smiled and then offered her his arm. "Since we are at the ball together, Lady Temperance, might you walk with me around the room? It would be of interest to me to see which of the other gentry are present."

She nodded and took his arm at once, not so much as glancing at Lord Barlington again. She heard him make some sort of guttural exclamation, something deep in his throat, but she did not so much as throw him a look. Instead, she felt her heart fill with a great and almost overwhelming respect and affection for this gentleman, the one who had – yet again – protected her from Lord Barlington. Not only that, he had given her the courage to speak openly, honestly and firmly and, in doing so, had helped her push Lord Barlington as far back as she could.

Whether Lord Barlington would be willing to give up as yet, she did not know.

Chapter Twenty

"How are you finding the evening?"

James grinned at Lord Thurston. "I think it is an excellent evening thus far. I have been able to see Lady Temperance push Lord Barlington away and have seen the frustration in his expression when he has been unable to get what he wants. I believe that he hoped this ball would bring them back together again, that they would, somehow, find a way to return to the close acquaintance they once had. Now, however, it surely *must* be clear to him that such a thing is not meant to be! She has rejected him –"

"And accepted you," Lord Thurston interrupted, his eyes twinkling as James' grin grew wider. "You are aware of that, are you not? There is clearly a connection between you, something which neither of you seem to have spoken of as yet but which is very obvious to not only myself but also to my wife."

"I think very well of Lady Temperance, if that is what you mean," James answered, only for his friend to guffaw and whack him on the arm. "Very well, very well! Yes, I will admit that there is... something... within my heart, though I do not know what it is."

"Affection?" Lord Thurston tilted his head. "Love?"

The word struck James hard in the chest but he did not immediately agree. Instead, he only ran one hand over his chin and considered. He had always been someone who gave great consideration to almost everything that he either thought or felt and this was no different.

"She has said that she is contented in her situation, as I am sure I have said to you before."

"Ah, but you have not offered her a *different* future from the one she is presently contented with," Lord Thurston interrupted. "She may be contented, yes, but that does not mean she is happy. It may very well be that what *she* is hoping for, is that you might be truthful about your own affections and step into the void which she has still within her heart."

James pressed his lips tight together for a moment, the music of the ball continuing to swirl around him. He had danced only once with Lady Temperance already and the second dance, the waltz, was still to come. His heart was filled with an excitement, an anticipation of what it would be like to hold the lady in his arms. What was such an emotion, such a sensation? Was it love? The very beginning, the first strains of such a deep and all-encompassing emotion?

"Do not think of it too long, else you will find yourself quite tied up in knots," Lord Thurston laughed, reaching out to take a brandy from the nearby table and handing it to James. "If you have an affection for her, then why do you not speak to her father and ask for his permission to court her? It might show the Duke of Danfield that he will not have to force his daughter to wed a gentleman she does not care for in the least."

Considering all of this, James shook his head. "I should like to speak with the Duke of Danfield, were I to do such a thing, but I think I should first like to ask Lady Temperance herself. After all, there is very little reason for me to ask her father about such a thing if she herself would not be willing to accept me!"

Lord Thurston's smile grew broad. "I am sure that she will accept you regardless of your worries."

"You cannot be sure of that."

His friend shrugged. "Mayhap but I can tell you what I see when she looks at you. I can see the tenderness in her smile, the hope in her eyes. If that is not reason to believe that she will accept you, then I do not know what is." He spread out his hands. "What reason do you have to hold back?"

James took in a deep breath, then lifted his shoulders and let them fall. "No reason at all, I suppose."

"And you are still to dance with her again?"

James nodded. "The waltz."

Immediately, Lord Thurston threw his head back and laughed. "Well, if that does not give her a hint that you might find her more than a mere acquaintance, I cannot imagine what else would be required! Indeed, Calverton, there is nothing more that you need to do, nothing that should hold you back. I think it would be excellent for you to pursue Lady Temperance. It would bring a great deal of happiness to you both."

After a moment, James lifted his glass of brandy in a half-toast, seeing his friend grin with the awareness that he was quite right. "Yes, I think that you must be right," he said, with a small, half smile. "Thank you, Thurston. I think tomorrow, I shall do just that."

***

"I am certain you will not have forgotten how to waltz, Lady Temperance." James smiled as he took her hand, the other settling at her waist. "Are you anxious? You do not have to be, I assure you."

Lady Temperance's smile wobbled, uncertainty jumping into her eyes. "I am a little concerned, yes. As I have said, it has been some years since I have waltzed."

"Then hold tight to me and I shall lead you," he promised, looking deeply into her eyes and finding his heart ricocheting around his chest. "There is nothing that you need to fear, I assure you."

The music began and, with Lady Temperance's hand rather tight on his own, James began to waltz. Their steps were quickly in time together and the longer they danced, the more Lady Temperance seemed to relax. Her fingers were no longer squeezing his, there came a small smile to her face and her eyes were no longer round with concern.

"We dance very well together, Lady Temperance," James murmured, seeing her eyes meld to his. "There was nothing for you to be concerned about at all."

"It seems not," she answered, as the music continued to whirl them around. "When it comes to you, Lord Calverton, it seems as though I am quite safe."

He smiled gently. "Of course you are safe."

The way she looked at him, the sheer joy of having her in his arms and the memory of all that Lord Thurston had advised made James' heart leap with a sudden hope and expectation. When the dance came to an end, James stepped back to bow, only to offer her his arm which she took without hesitation.

"Another short turn about the room?"

She nodded.

"There is something I should like to ask you, Lady Temperance," James began, before his own fears could prevent him from speaking. "Though I understand that, as you yourself told me only a short while ago, you are very contented with your situation at present. If you do not wish to change your situation, then I quite understand but – "

"What is it that you mean, Lord Calverton?"

James looked to her, seeing her green eyes rounding a little, though he could not tell whether it was from anticipation or concern.

"I would like to court you."

The words came out a little more bluntly than he had anticipated and James quickly pulled his gaze from hers, continuing to walk around the room with slow steps rather than looking at her. He did not know what it was that she felt, did not know what her reaction was going to be and his fears began to mount with every moment that passed.

"I – I do not know what to say."

James forced himself to look at her. "Lady Temperance, there is no requirement nor expectation for you to consent. I understand that you are very contented as you are, and therefore, if this is not something that would please you, then I quite understand. I will continue to be your friend and I will continue to defend you from Lord Barlington, regardless of what your answer may be."

"Oh, Lord Calverton, you cannot know what this means to me."

Coming to a stop and unable to bear the not knowing any longer, James turned to look at her directly. "Whatever you desire, Lady Temperance. That is all that I want."

Her smile grew and sent light into her eyes. "I want nothing more than to accept," she said, delight evident in both her voice and her expression. "Thank you for asking me. I find myself rather overwhelmed by it, truth be told!"

James swallowed hard, struggling to know what to say. He himself felt the very same as Lady Temperance, overwhelmed with relief, joy and delight. "I – I shall still speak to your father, of course."

Lady Temperance smiled back at him. "I am certain he will accept your request. Thank you again, Lord Calverton. This has made my evening truly wonderful when I was certain that it would be nothing but a night to endure!"

"I feel the very same way," he told her, taking her hand and bowing over it, his smile growing, his heart flooding with happiness. "And just as soon as I am able, I shall speak to your father and all will be well. I am quite sure of it."

Chapter Twenty-One

"Temperance?"

Setting down her paintbrush, Temperance turned toward her mother. "Yes, Mama?"

"Lord Barlington has come to call," the Duchess told her, a flash in her eyes. "You will speak with him for a few minutes and then I will return to join you. He tells me that he has been unable to tell you all that is on his heart and I have promised him that he can do so now."

"And I refuse," Temperance replied, firmly. "I have no desire to hear what he has to say. I have already spoken to my father about another matter and – "

"The Earl?" The Duchess let out a broken laugh and shook her head. "You have a *Marquess* seeking you out, Temperance!"

"And I do not care for him!" Temperance exclaimed. "Do you not understand by now, Mama, that – "

"That is *enough*, Temperance!" The Duchess threw up her hands, her voice echoing around the room. "You *will* see Lord Barlington and you *will* listen to him or so help me, there will be heavy consequences!"

Temperance blinked, a little shocked at her mother's vehemence but there was no time for her to say anything more. Her mother marched from the room but the moment she stepped out, Lord Barlington made his way in. The smile on his face made Temperance's heart sink low and she quickly resumed her place behind the couch, ready to protect herself from him if she had to.

"It seems clear to me that you do not want to speak with me, Temperance."

"*Lady* Temperance," she answered, fully aware that he would have heard everything she had just said to her mother – and what response the Duchess had given. "No, I do not. I have no knowledge as to why you insist but it seems as though I have no choice." She shrugged lightly, keeping her tone as unconcerned as she could. "Not that such things matter. If I listen to you, then my mother will be satisfied, you will have said whatever it is you wish to say and that will be that."

Lord Barlington chuckled and Temperance's skin crawled. How much she despised this gentleman! Could she truly have thought herself in love with him so long ago? Perhaps she had never truly known him, had never really understood his character.

"Tell me what you are thinking, Temperance," he said, coming to stand only a few steps away from her though the couch remained in between them. "Your eyes are thoughtful. I have always loved your eyes."

Her jaw tightened. "I am thinking how glad I am for *this*," she said, throwing up one hand towards her scar. "It is something that, at one time, tore me apart but now, I find myself glad of it."

"Glad?" Lord Barlington snorted. "How could you find yourself happy over such a marring of your features? What sort of joy can that ugliness bring you?"

Anger burst through her and she squeezed her hands tight into fists, refusing to permit his harsh words to elicit a lack of propriety from her. She would remain in control, regardless of what he threw at her.

"It brings me joy because it has shown me precisely the sort of gentleman you are," she said, softly. "I am glad of it because it saved me from a life of what would have been nothing short of misery. I would have married you, believing you to be the gentleman you pretended to be, only to realise that you were not that fellow at all. How glad I am now that our engagement broke apart! How relieved I am to know that I shall be free of you forever."

Lord Barlington's jaw set, his eyes turning to granite. "I would not say such a thing as that," he said, his voice dropping low as a light shiver ran over Temperance's skin. "I have decided that we shall marry, Temperance."

She shook her head. "In case I have not made myself clear, Barlington, I shall *never* marry you. I have no interest in reacquainting myself with you, no interest in even hearing what you have to say. So – "

"If you do not, then I shall bring heavy consequences down upon Lord Calverton."

In an instant, all of Temperance's confidence evaporated. Her eyes flared wide and she stared at Lord Barlington, seeing how he smirked. Did he know what she felt for Lord Calverton? Were his threats something she ought to truly consider?

"I saw you waltzing with him last evening," Lord Barlington continued, coming around the couch though Temperance, on weak legs, did her best to move away from him. "I saw him speaking with you and how much you smiled at him. What was it that he asked you, Temperance? Did he ask to court you? To further his acquaintance with you? Well no, you shall not be permitted to step into his arms, I am afraid. That pleasure belongs to me."

Temperance's throat ached but, with fire still burning in her veins – albeit without the same strength – she glared back at him. "It is nothing to do with you what I spoke of with Lord Calverton. But your threats mean nothing to me, Barlington. Nothing at all."

"No?" His eyebrow lifted as though he knew she was lying.

"No," she answered, as firmly as she could. "I do not believe you. Even if you did threaten such things, I shall simply speak of them to Lord Calverton and then what will you do?"

He lifted his shoulders. "I think I should carry out my threat regardless," he answered, coldly. "There are easy enough rumours to spread about any one person of the *ton* and whether the person knows of them or not makes no difference. It will be up to the *ton* to decide whether they are true."

Temperance blinked. "Rumours? You intend to start rumours about Lord Calverton?" She rolled her eyes, attempting to cling onto a little strength. "That means nothing."

"Oh, but it does. He has suffered a great deal already, has he not?" Evidently seeing her confusion, Lord Barlington let out a bark of laughter. "He has not told you of it! Well then, permit me to do so. You see, my dear Temperance, Lord Calverton is the *younger* brother. The elder brother, the one who first claimed the title, was nothing but a rogue and a scoundrel, who wasted his fortune on all the things a gentleman ought not even to consider. He died in a most tragic manner – but it certainly did bring with it a lot of whispers and gossip with it. The *ton* are very interested in that particular family and would, I dare say, love to know that Lord Calverton is exactly like his brother, if not worse!"

Tears began to prick in the corner of Temperance's eyes. "But he is not."

Lord Barlington laughed again. "I am well aware of that but to ruin his reputation would bring me a great deal of pleasure. And, mayhap, I shall do the very same to Lady Calverton. And mayhap, after that, the same to Lord and Lady Thurston."

Temperance began to shake violently, aware that everything Lord Barlington was saying had a ring of truth to it. She could not speak. She could not find a single word to say to him in response, her breathing ragged and quick.

"You see, my dear Temperance, unless I am permitted to marry you, I will do all of these things – and more," Lord Barlington murmured, though he did not move towards her. Instead, his eyes set to hers, the darkness there frightening her all the more. "Your sisters will not be safe from me. Do you hear me?"

What could she do but nod?

"I *will* have you, Temperance," he finished, his voice low and thick with wickedness. "I must."

"But why?" she whispered, tears beginning to fall to her cheeks. "Why must you do such a thing? What is it about me that forces such schemes?"

Lord Barlington waved a hand, half turning away from her. "Oh, it is not you, Lady Temperance," he said, with a snort of evident derision. "I have every intention of setting you aside, to have you live in a private quarter of the house for I certainly have no desire to look upon your countenance every day! Though there will have to be the heir produced, of course. That is a requirement. But I also require your dowry and the income that you will bring to this marriage." He tilted his head at her. "That is all."

Temperance closed her eyes and shuddered violently. She could barely breathe, her heart racing, her mind screaming at her to find an answer, to find a way of escape.

She could find none.

"I will go and tell you father that we are reconciled and will marry within the month," she heard Lord Barlington say, his voice sounding both very near and very distant, both at the same time. "I do warn you now, Temperance. If you dare say a word of this to anyone, if you dare tell Lord Calverton of my threats, they will come down upon every single person you care for without hesitation. Lives will be ruined. Your nieces and nephews will have no reputation to speak of. Can you live with that?"

The door opened and closed and Temperance dropped her head, her shoulders rounding as she broke into sobs. What was she to do? She could find no way of escape, no way to break free from Lord Barlington's grip.

But what of Lord Calverton? her heart wailed. *What of what you feel for him? What of the affection you have within your heart?*

That made her heart tear all over again and, blindly, she made her way back to the couch, sitting down heavily and, her shoulders shaking, gave in to her grief.

"Temperance?"

She did not look up.

"Temperance! Goodness, whatever has happened?"

An arm went around her shoulders, her aunt's voice murmuring words of comfort but Temperance heard nothing other than the tremulous beating of her heart, feeling nothing but the pain of her world shattering all over again.

Chapter Twenty-Two

"Your Grace. Thank you for seeing me." James inclined his head as the Duke of Danfield nodded. "I presume you know why I have come to speak with you?"

"I do, though I must tell you that something has transpired." Without saying anything more, the Duke of Danfield handed James a glass with brandy in it, a suggestion, mayhap, that James would require such sustenance soon enough.

"I see." James took the seat to which the Duke gestured and, his stomach beginning to churn suddenly, looked back at the Duke in question. He did not understand what could have gone wrong. It had only been two days since the ball and, given that Lady Temperance had already agreed to his courtship – and had, no doubt, spoken to her father about it – he did not understand why there would be anything of concern. "Please, what it is?"

The Duke of Danfield shook his head and sighed, looking away from James. "Two days ago, Lord Calverton, I had my daughter coming to speak with me about you. She told me that you had expressed an interest in courting her and that she would very much like to accept you."

James smiled, remembering that wonderful moment. "Yes, it was at the ball. I know that I should have spoken to you beforehand but – "

"No, no, do not concern yourself with that." The Duke's frown lingered as he sat forward, looking at James with sharp eyes. "My daughter was nothing but delighted, Lord Calverton. I gave her my consent, telling her that I was truly thrilled to hear of your desire and she practically danced out of the room."

James' smile grew wider. "I am very glad to hear it, Your Grace."

"However," the Duke continued, seeming not to hear James, "yesterday, I was informed that Lord Barlington's proposal to my daughter has been accepted."

All of his breath left his body in one moment. James could barely take a breath, everything in him growing suddenly cold.

"I do not know what to make of it, if I am truthful," the Duke continued, quietly. "Lord Calverton, I am mayhap speaking a little out of turn but given that you seem to care for my daughter, I shall tell you honestly. There is something about this that does not seem right to me."

James, blinking, threw back his brandy and let the heat of it steal away some of the cold in his chest. He could not quite take in everything the Duke was saying, struggling to comprehend all that was being told to him.

"My daughter has been white faced and sorrowful ever since I was informed of this engagement." The Duke leaned forward in his chair, his eyes fixed to James. "I do not believe that she has accepted him willingly and though I have asked her about it, she simply says that it is just as she wants."

"I cannot believe that," James replied, hoarsely. "I *will not* believe it."

"Good." The Duke slapped his knee, making James start in surprise at the noise. "Mayhap she will speak with you."

"Do you know where she might be?" James asked, a sudden desperation coursing through him. "I must see her. I must speak with her, I do not understand why... " Dropping his head forward, he pushed his fingers through his hair. "I do not understand."

The Duke let out a long breath. "It is most grievous a thing for me to see. My wife – " He stopped short as James looked up, his eyes a little rounded. With another sigh, he continued. "My wife has long been insistent that the Marquess of Barlington is the best choice for our daughter. She was not particularly pleased to hear that *you* had decided to pursue Temperance, nor that Temperance had been eager to accept!"

"I presume then, without speaking out of turn, that she is pleased at this engagement?"

The Duke nodded, not appearing to be at all upset in hearing James speak so. "Yes, she is thrilled. I, however, see my daughter's sorrow and find my heart filled with worry for her. As I have said, I have tried speaking with her and she has not told me a single thing."

"Then I will do my best to find out the truth," James said quickly, getting to his feet. "I cannot fathom the reasoning behind her desire to accept him! Lord Barlington, from what I knew, was practically loathed by her, though I do not want to speak out of turn."

The Duke scowled. "You do not speak out of turn, Lord Calverton. The reason I asked my daughter to reconsider him was truly because I was concerned for her. I did not want her to sit here, in this place, and feel herself entirely alone for years and years without end. I did not know if she was happy here, if the situation would be one of joy for her – and then, I thought that if Lord Barlington was sincere, then that might offer her a fresh start, a chance to be settled and have a family of her own. Do not for a moment think that I was at all delighted by Lord Barlington's return! I found his manner arrogant, his expression of interest towards my daughter to be less than sincere and yet, with my wife's eager encouragement, I found myself willing to give Temperance the opportunity to hear the gentleman's apology, at the very least."

"You do not need to explain yourself to me, Your Grace," James replied his heart still pounding rather furiously. "I quite understand – though I am glad that you feel the very same way about Lord Barlington as I!"

"Then go to her," came the Duke's fervent response. "See if you can find a way to convince her to step away from Lord Barlington once and for all."

"I shall." James dropped into a bow, panic beginning to tighten around his chest. "Good afternoon, Your Grace. I hope I shall return with good news."

"As do I."

***

"Lady Hartford?" James caught the arm of the lady, making her turn towards him. "Lady Hartford, I must ask if you know where Lady Temperance has gone."

"Oh, Lord Calverton." Lady Hartford's eyes swelled with tears though she blinked them back quickly. "You must know by now that – "

"I know everything but I do not believe that she has consented to this willingly."

Lady Hartford's throat bobbed as she swallowed hard. "She was greatly distraught," she whispered, her eyes closing for a moment. "I came into the room only a few minutes after Lord Barlington had taken his leave and she was nothing but tears. She sobbed and could not be comforted – and yet when I asked her about what had happened, she would say nothing."

"Nothing at all?"

Lady Hartford shook her head. "Nothing," she said again, her voice wobbling. "You must understand, Lord Calverton, my niece and I have shared a great many things since she first arrived here. The fact that she will not speak to me about anything, that she will not say a single word about what took place between Lord Barlington and herself breaks my heart!"

"I want to speak with her," James told the lady, as she grasped his hand and pressed it tightly. "I must know what has taken place. We were to be courting, you understand, and now, only two days after she gave me her consent, I find her engaged to Lord Barlington? It does not make sense."

"Especially since she despises the gentleman," Lady Hartford muttered, darkly. "He has done something to her, I know of it. I just do not know *what* it is."

"He is an unscrupulous fellow," James agreed. "But I will find her and I will speak with her. I can only hope that she will tell me the truth so that we can aid her in bringing this to an end."

Lady Hartford nodded, her eyes glistening. "I know that you want her happiness," she whispered, her voice breaking. "As do I. I think she is at the shore, Lord Calverton."

"Then I will go there at once." Releasing her hand, he nodded to her. "Pray that all will be well, Lady Hartford. For I have nothing else but that."

Chapter Twenty-Three

For the first time in her life, the wind and the waves did nothing to comfort her. Temperance stood on the shoreline, her vision blurring as fresh tears burned in her eyes. Even now, a day after Lord Barlington had made his demands, she still felt the shock and the sting of it just as fiercely as she had done at the time. It burned through her, stealing away her joy, stealing away any sense of happiness for her future and instead, leaving her with nothing but darkness.

But I care for Lord Calverton, she thought to herself, tears dripping to her cheeks. *When he asked to court me, it was as though every single moment of pain had been swallowed up and was gone. I had hope. I had happiness. I had... did I have love?*

Her eyes closed tightly as tears began to drip to her cheeks. The wind blew at them as though it was seeking to push them from her, to help soften the pain but more came in their place. She wrapped her arms around herself, dropping her head forward, wishing desperately that she could find a solution to what Lord Barlington had forced upon her but nothing came.

If I truly care for Lord Calverton as I do, if there really is the whisper of love within my heart for him, then I will not step back from this. I must protect him, whatever the cost to me.

"Temperance!"

Her name was on the wind and Temperance shuddered, too afraid to look around for fear that it was Lord Barlington coming to haunt her again.

"Temperance, please!"

A hand went to her arm and Temperance flinched, pulling her arm away and stumbling back. "Leave me!"

She turned sharply, ready to strike out at Lord Barlington only to see Lord Calverton looking back at her.

Weakness flooded her. "Calverton."

"Temperance," he said again, his voice softer now, his eyes searching hers as he reached for her hands. "Temperance, please. Tell me what has happened."

She shook her head, wordlessly.

"This is not what you want. I know it. *You* know it," he told her, as she dropped her head, unable to look into his eyes. "What has happened, Temperance? Why did you accept him?"

His hands pressed hers and tears fell to her cheeks all over again. "I have no choice, Calverton," she whispered, her voice broken with emotion. "Please, do not try to dissuade me. I must accept."

"Why must you?" he begged, coming closer to her. "You accepted *me,* I know that you wanted to begin our courtship. What did he say to you to force you to accept him? I do not understand."

The urge to tell him everything grew so strong, Temperance had to close her eyes to shut out the sight of his handsome, earnest face. "Please, Calverton."

"I will not leave you until you tell me."

Her eyes flew open, shock racing through her.

"I will not give up. You have become too precious to me, too dear for me to permit you to marry the very gentleman who caused you so much pain. Especially when I know that it is against your will."

Temperance looked back at him, not knowing what she ought to do. Lord Calverton gazed back at her, then dropped one of her hands and for a moment, she thought he was to step away. Then his hand lifted to her cheek, his thumb brushing lightly across her skin as he chased the tears away.

"Tell me the truth, Temperance, please. I beg of you, please be truthful. There is nothing that he can do that will – "

"But there is!"

The words flew out of her mouth before she could prevent them and Temperance clapped one hand to her mouth, only to then try and turn away from him, twisting out of his grip.

"Temperance!" Lord Calverton caught her around the waist as she began to sob, his hands going to frame her face, his eyes searching desperately for the truth. "What was it he said? What has he threatened?"

Temperance closed her eyes again, her breath shuddering out of her. "If I tell you, then what he has threatened will come to pass."

"He will not know you have told me," Lord Calverton promised, as Temperance opened her eyes, only for a sudden fear to clutch at her heart. Again, she spun away from him, her hand pressing against her heart, dread pouring into her veins. Her eyes scanned the cliffs, her breathing ragged as she searched for any sign of Lord Barlington.

"Temperance, come back!" Lord Calverton proved to her that he was not about to be dismissed, rushing after her so that, no matter how many steps she took, he was always there, following after her. "What is it that you are so afraid of?"

"He could be watching!" Temperance cried, her heart pounding. "He could see us and then – "

Lord Calverton caught her hand and then, after a moment, began to pull her towards the edge of the cliffs. "Come here," he encouraged, urgently. "We will stand here in the shadows so we cannot be seen by anyone. And then, you *must* tell me the truth, Temperance. I cannot leave you in this state."

Temperance went with him, her heart quailing still, her eyes still searching the top of the cliffs. Did she dare be honest with him? Did she dare tell him everything that Lord Barlington had threatened?

"Now." Lord Calverton, his breathing a little quicker now, turned to face her and captured her hands in his again. "Now, we are safe. We cannot be seen and I assure you, Temperance, I will say nothing to Lord Barlington of what you have told me. Whatever it is, I will find another way to free you from this engagement *without* telling him that I know of his threats."

Temperance shuddered violently.

"You can trust me," Lord Calverton said softly, coming to stand a little closer to her as the wind continued to whistle around them. "Both your father *and* your aunt are deeply concerned for you, my dear Temperance, as am I. They know that you are unhappy. They want to know what is wrong and neither of them want to see you marry Lord Barlington."

Temperance closed her eyes in an attempt to steady herself. She took in a deep breath, then let it out again. "If I do not marry Lord Barlington, then everyone I love is in danger of being completely and utterly ruined." Opening her eyes, she looked back at him. "Yourself included."

"Ruined?"

She nodded, the words coming a little more easily now. "He told me about your brother and his untimely passing, as well as the rumours which have pursued you and your family since then. He told me how you would be entirely ruined should he begin to whisper about you to the *ton.*"

Lord Calverton's jaw tightened.

"And then he has threatened your mother, my dear friend Lady Thurston and even my own sisters! I dare not do anything other than obey him for I care about you too much to let that happen." Tears began to prick the corners of her eyes as Lord Calverton's expression softened. "It is to protect you, to protect *everyone* that I must do this."

Lord Calverton shook his head. "No, Lady Temperance. It is not your responsibility to protect me."

"But if I do anything other than this, even if I tell anyone about what he has said, then he will begin those threats!" Her voice rising as panic began to flood through her. "I must protect you all. I must – "

Lord Calverton's arms were suddenly around her waist and before she could move, before she could react, his mouth was on hers and she was pulled tight against him.

The fear she felt, the dread, the worry and the concern all faded into nothingness. Instead, she was left with a feeling of relief, of ever growing happineness. It burst through her like fireworks, sending heat into every part of her being until there was nothing she could do but cling to him.

"I am sorry." Lord Calverton broke their kiss somewhat abruptly, pulling back rather sharply. "I did not mean to – that is to say… "

"Please do not apologise." Temperance let out a small, broken laugh as she closed her eyes for a moment. "I do not think I could bear that."

"Then I shall not." Lord Calverton's voice was gentle, one hand going to her chin as she looked back into his eyes. "Temperance, I care for you. I believe that I am half in love with you already! I do not want you to suffer, I do not want you to bear a burden that is not yours to carry. If you will permit me, I will find a way to break this engagement and to have Lord Barlington's wickedness shown to all who know him."

Temperance could not bring herself to believe it. It seemed too good to be true, too wonderful a prospect. "I do not think you can, Lord Calverton. His threats are too many, his strength too great."

Lord Calverton shook his head. "No, it is not. I will find a way. I will not be alone in this. Lord Thurston will be of aid to me."

Again, fear clutched at Temperance's heart. "I am afraid that he will find out, that my friend's good name will be ruined!"

"Can you trust me?"

The question quietened her and, as she looked back into Lord Calverton's eyes, Temperance felt her heart begin to piece back together.

"Yes," she breathed, after only a few moments. "Yes, I think that I can."

"My heart is filled with nothing but affection for you, Temperance," he told her, his face only a few inches from her own. "I cannot help but care for you. Even if you did not return my affections, I would do anything I could to prevent you from stepping forward into the unhappiness that you would be sure to get from any future with Lord Barlington."

Tears began to burn in Temperance's eyes, her happiness beginning to flood through her, chasing away the sorrow, the anxiety and the dread which she had carried with her. "But I care for you in return, Calverton. I had never dreamed that such a thing might be, I thought I would be contented to live out my years here, alone with my aunt and uncle, but instead... instead, you have offered me such a happiness that it tore my heart into pieces to think it was now taken from me."

"It has *not* been taken from you." The fervency with which he spoke made Temperance tremble but this time, it came from sheer joy rather than fright. When he leaned down, she was ready for him, kissing him back with a sweetness which tore through her without hesitation. It made her heart sing, her joy complete as she leaned into him. She trusted him, trusted that he would be able to do as he had promised and, as he wrapped his arms tight around her, Temperance knew she was safe.

Lord Barlington would not succeed. Her future was no longer dark. She had Lord Calverton's word and that was all that she needed.

Chapter Twenty-Four

"I should call him out."

James shook his head as his friend marched up and down the drawing room, his teeth gritted. "That would do no good, my friend, though I quite understand the sentiment."

"My poor, dear Temperance," Lady Thurston breathed, her face rather pale. "I cannot believe she has endured so much!"

"It seems that the Duchess is quite contented with it all, though I do not think that she is aware of the Marquess' threats," James replied, finding his anger burning hot as he thought of what the Duchess had done, albeit unwittingly. "She is so determined for her daughter to marry the very highest title that she has not realized the darkness of his character."

"Then what are we to do?" Lord Thurston demanded, stopping for a moment and throwing up his hands. "If we call him out, then we have a chance of putting this to an end... permanently."

Again, James shook his head. "I would surmise that the gentleman would make his escape and then go directly to London, where he would do as he has threatened."

"And all would be lost." Lady Thurston passed one hand over her eyes. "Goodness, the man is very wickedness itself!"

"I would agree. Therefore, it is imperative that we find a way to prove that to all who know him. A way where we can take what we have learned and pass it to the *ton* so that he is rejected – and so that anything he says thereafter will be ignored, thereby wiping his threats of strength." He eyed his friend carefully, relieved when Lord Thurston finally began to nod. "I think that we must ask Sir Jeffries."

Lord Thurston's eyes flared. "The knight?"

"Yes, recall that we saw him in conversation with Lord Barlington," James reminded him. "We did not know what they were arguing about but it was clear that there was *some* sort of altercation there."

Slowly, Lord Thurston began to nod. "Yes, that is a wise idea."

"Lady Temperance told me that the only reason Lord Barlington seeks to marry her is, as he stated himself, because of her dowry and the income she will bring to the marriage. Does that mean that he is not financially sound?"

"It may be," Lady Thurston agreed. "But you will have to have evidence of that. Saying anything to him is much too risky."

"So we will find Sir Jeffries and speak to him," Lord Thurston said, gesturing to James to rise. "Now?"

James nodded. "Now, if that pleases you. I know it is a little late in the evening but I could not wait until the morrow. Once Lady Temperance returned home, I thought only about coming here and telling you both all that I knew."

"Of course, you must both go at once and with the greatest urgency." Lady Thurston took her husband's hand and looked straight into his eyes. "Do be careful, however. It is clear that Lord Barlington is a very evil man."

"I will be." Lord Thurston kissed his wife's hand and, after a moment, stepped away. James followed quickly after him and, in only a few minutes, both gentlemen were on their horses, riding across the moor to Lord Jeffries' house.

****

"The tavern is *not* where I expected a knight of the realm to be residing!" James jumped down from his horse, grimacing at the noise and jocularity which came from the tavern. "I thought he might be a little more respectable than to be present at this hour!"

Lord Thurston offered him a small, wry smile. "You would be surprised, my friend. There is very little by way of expectation in this small, quiet part of England. Though I myself would not spend time here in the evenings, it is understandable to me that a Knight or a Baron might do so."

James pulled his mouth to one side, a little frustrated that they had been directed here. To his mind, he was sure that Sir Jeffries would be already well into his cups and would be unable to give them any sort of aid, though Lord Thurston seemed to be a little more hopeful.

"Even if he is a little tipsy, it may be that the liquor will loosen his tongue a little more," Lord Thurston suggested, seemingly able to read James' thoughts as they tied up their horses. "Come now, let us go inside without too much pomp.

Those within the tavern are bound to notice our presence and we do not want them to react by falling into silence now, do we?" So saying, he took off his jacket and his hat and set his jacket on top of his saddle, his hat on the gate beside them. Looking to James to do the same, he lifted an eyebrow but without question or hesitation, James followed suit, eschewing his gloves also. No doubt his hat would be a little dusty – or mayhap disappeared entirely by some ragamuffin with sticky fingers – but he did not have time nor the inclination to care about that. The only person on his mind was Lady Temperance and the happiness he wanted to restore her to.

"Come, then." With a set of his shoulders, James cleared his throat and made his way towards the tavern. Pushing open the door, he and Lord Thurston stepped inside but, much to his relief, only a few of those within looked at them. There were a good many bodies present, the air thick and warm as the candles and lamps flickered a dull light across the room. There was a great deal of raucous laughter and, as James' eyes adjusted, he caught sight of the very man they were looking for. Sir Jeffries was seated at the back of the room, sitting at a table with a few cards in his hand. Evidently, he was in the middle of a card game.

"Look. There." James made to step forward, only for Lord Thurston to let out a hiss of breath and catch his arm. About to question what his friend was doing, James caught sight of a familiar face and the words died on his lips.

Lord Barlington was present.

"Whatever is *he* doing here?" James muttered, as he and Lord Thurston watched the gentleman closely. "Is he playing cards with Sir Jeffries?" He frowned, hard. "A Marquess playing cards with a Knight, in a dull, dark village tavern?"

"He wants Lady Temperance's dowry and income, does he not?" Lord Thurston gestured to the man. "Mayhap this is why."

Anger began to burn in the pit of James' stomach, his lip curling and his stomach twisting hard as he glared at the fellow, though Lord Barlington did not so much as glance in his direction.

"Wait, my friend." Again, Lord Thurston held him back. "Why do we not simply watch and wait?"

"Because I do not want to!" James exclaimed. "I want to go to Sir Jeffries, demand to speak with him and mayhap, in doing so, demand to know what the Marquess is doing here also!"

"But he will not tell you and you will only raise his suspicions if you do such a thing," his friend warned. "Listen to me. First, we must send a note to the Duke himself, asking him to come to join us. Thereafter, we must wait until Lord Barlington has imbibed a little more, until the liquor has dulled his mind a little. *That* way, he will be more than willing to tell us all that we need to know. The Marquess will tell us of his guilt without our use of force, I am sure of it."

"And if he does not?"

Lord Thurston smiled ruefully. "At least we will have tried the gentler way. Recall, we must be cautious. Our questions must not be laden with anger, our voices must be calm and even jovial. Anything else could arouse his suspicions, despite the brandy in his veins!"

As much as James wanted to rush forward, sit down at the table and start throwing questions at both the gentlemen, he slowly began to realize that his friend was right. Closing his eyes tightly for a moment, he took in a long, slow breath to steady himself, and then nodded.

"Very well."

Lord Thurston nodded. "Good. Now, let us go and get ourselves a drink and sit down so we may watch the game from a distance." He slapped James on the shoulder. "Do not worry, my friend. It will not be long now."

***

"Lord Barlington? Is that you?" James sat down in a chair just behind the Marquess, forcing the gentleman to look over his shoulder. The man was so addled, however, he swayed heavily in his seat, clutching at the table so as to right himself.

"It is," he said, a jovial tone to his voice which told James that he had not yet been recognized. With a nod, he watched as the Duke of Danfield and Lord Thurston came to join him, though they made certain to stand behind the Marquess also, keeping their presence hidden from him as best they could. The arrival of the Duke had caused something of a stir within the tavern itself but given that Lord Barlington had imbibed a good deal more brandy than when James had first arrived, he had not even noticed. That had been of great relief to James and all he needed now was for

Lord Barlington to confess the truth so that this great and terrible nightmare might come to an end.

"How good to see you again," James continued, his tone as warm and as friendly as he could muster. "It has been a very pleasant evening, has it not? Tell me, have you had any success this evening?"

Sir Jeffries snorted, before Lord Barlington had a chance to answer. "Certainly, he has not! It is just the same as before."

"Before?" Lord Thurston asked, making Lord Barlington swivel around in his chair, though he then swayed so heavily, he had to grip onto the table with great force so as to steady himself.

"Yes, just as before," Sir Jeffries said loudly, catching Lord Barlington's attention again. "The gentleman has been in this tavern almost every evening since he arrived, attempting to regain the coin he has lost." He made a face. "Alas, he proves time and again that he is not the sort of gentleman who is *able* to play cards well, given the amount he imbibes!"

James threw a glance to Lord Thurston and the Duke of Danfield but said nothing more. Lord Thurston lifted an eyebrow as the Duke's expression grew rather dark. Evidently, this display of drunkenness from Lord Barlington was less than impressive.

"I have not lost *too* much," Lord Barlington laughed, though his voice grew a little whiny. "And I have said I will repay it all."

"With what coin?" Sir Jeffries asked, sounding as though he did not believe a word of what Lord Barlington had said. "You have already told me that you lack coin at the present moment. How are you going to repay your debt to me? Though," he continued, with a roll of his eyes, "I myself am foolish for continuing to play with you when you have not yet paid what you already owe me!"

James hesitated, wondering if he dared be bold and ask Lord Barlington something a little more personal. Considering, he then chose to redirect his question to Sir Jeffries, hoping it might encourage Lord Barlington to interject. "How much are you owed, Sir Jeffries? I am sure it cannot be too great for a Marquess to pay!"

Lord Barlington snorted, his lip curling. "I am sure it will not be."

"I have heard you say that before and yet, you are still unable to pay me!" Sir Jeffries exclaimed, as Lord Barlington rolled his eyes. "I have no assurances."

"Well, you may have one now." Lord Barlington's fist thumped down onto the table, making James jump in surprise. "I am to marry very soon and once I have received her dowry and the income she will bring, then I will be more than able to pay whatever debts I have incurred. There, now, does that satisfy you?"

A coldness wrapped around James' heart as he looked back at the Duke of Danfield, seeing a red flush begin to creep up the Duke's face. He himself had very little thought as to what he ought to say next, though he certainly felt the very same anger that he was sure was in the Duke's heart.

Attempting to keep his tone light, James spoke again. "Goodness, a Marquess who is a little impoverished! Whatever did you do to lose so much of your fortune?"

Lord Barlington did not answer, his shoulders dropping.

"It must have been something very grave indeed," Sir Jeffries chimed in, a heavy expression settling on his face. "Though you have not spoken to me of it as yet. I personally believe that the Marquess of Barlington is much too inclined towards cards and the like."

"That is the same as many a gentleman!" Lord Barlington exclaimed, speaking with a great fervency. "I am not the only one who enjoys such a thing, despite the fact that I have lost almost every game we have played."

"You have lost every game," Sir Jeffries corrected, with yet another roll of his eyes. "And yet you continue to play?"

"As I have said, I will be able to pay for all my debts very soon, once I have wed."

James scowled, rubbing one hand over his face to chase his thoughts away from Lord Barlington's selfish words. He knew now why the gentleman wanted to marry Lady Temperance: he was impoverished; a fact he had managed to hide from everyone. No doubt some of the *ton* knew of it – or *would* know of it, should he go to London – and news of that impoverished state would mean that no young lady would ever even be permitted to consider him! Thus, he had decided that the best thing for him to do was to wed Lady Temperance and, in doing so, be given her dowry and whatever income she would bring into the marriage. That was his answer to his present difficulties, it seemed, and the way he was using Lady Temperance made James' anger burn hot.

"I did not know you were to marry." Sir Jeffries tilted his head, placing a card out on the table and then arching an eyebrow at Lord Barlington. "Might I ask who the lady is? She must be very refined, I am sure, if she is to bring in such a substantial dowry."

Lord Barlington, rather than smile and agree, let out a long, heavy sigh as though even the thought of marrying the lady was a disappointing one. "The young lady may be refined but I confess, I struggle even to look at her for any length of time."

Anger sent shards of fury right into James' heart and he dropped his head, taking slow breaths so that he would not react and give himself away.

"Whatever do you mean?" Again, Sir Jeffries spoke, encouraging Lord Barlington to say more as James, Lord Thurston and the Duke simply listened. "I cannot imagine that you would tie yourself to someone such as that!"

"Oh, her face would frighten a horse!" Lord Barlington exclaimed, and in that instant, James found himself on his feet, a loud buzzing in his ears, his heart screaming at him as his hands curled into tight fists.

Lord Thurston's hand on his arm forced him to sit back down.

"I have told her plainly that she will live in a separate part of my manor house, for I do not want to look upon her countenance every day!" Lord Barlington laughed, throwing down a card seemingly without even looking at it. "She will be set away from me though I will *have* to do something about the heir. It will be best to do such a thing when it is dark, I suppose, for then I will not see her."

The heat in James' heart burned all the hotter and he closed his eyes for fear that, if he so much as looked at Lord Barlington for even a second longer, he would most certainly deliver him a proper thrashing.

"She knows full well that I only desire her wealth," Lord Barlington continued with a shrug. "There is nothing I am keeping from her in that."

"I am surprised that she still wishes to marry you!" Sir Jeffries shook his head and threw down another card, eyeing Lord Barlington's hand carefully. "I would have thought any young lady would have been rather displeased to marry a gentleman of such opinions."

Lord Barlington laughed and put another card out on the table. "You are quite correct there, Sir Jeffries! But there are ways and means of... *encouraging* such a connection, you understand?"

"Encouraging?"

James opened his eyes as Sir Jeffries continued to question Lord Barlington, clearly not realizing that he was helping James with his questions.

"Yes, encouragements, let us call them that." Lord Barlington laughed again and James gritted his teeth, hating the sound. "It is a very useful tool, Sir Jeffries. Stating exactly what you will do if the young lady does not accept you means that you are bound to gain exactly what you desire: namely, her hand in marriage, her dowry, her yearly income and relief from your present financial difficulties. Yes, it does mean that I have to have this scarred, rather ugly young lady as my wife but there are many distractions that a gentleman can have besides his wife! I think I shall do very well out of all of this, I must say."

If it had not been for Lord Thurston reaching out to restrain him yet again, James was quite certain he would have planted both hands around Lord Barlington's throat and squeezed. Instead, he rose from his chair and, somewhat blindly, made his way out of the tavern. His chest was tight, his breathing growing quick and fast as he fought hard to keep control. The cool evening air helped to quieten him a little but still, James began to pace, his hands squeezing tight, his breathing ragged, his whole body burning.

"Are you quite all right?" Lord Thurston hurried over to him, his hand going to James' shoulder. "The Duke is coming momentarily. He too is furious."

James nodded, coming to a stop. "I cannot believe the cruel words which came from his lips."

"He does not care for anyone aside from himself, it seems. To threaten the lady so is... repugnant."

"He will not be permitted to do such a thing."

James turned just as the Duke of Danfield came to join them; the dim lantern light illuminating his features a little and letting James see just how furious the man was.

"No wonder Temperance was too afraid to tell me what he had said," the Duke continued, rubbing one hand over his face. "From what Lord Barlington said, it seems that he threatened someone if she did not do as he asked."

"He threatened to ruin everyone she cares for, including her sisters, Lord and Lady Thurston, my mother and myself" James told him, seeing how the shadow on the Duke's face grew ever stronger. "She was afraid to even speak of what he had said, for I believe his threats were very severe indeed."

The Duke closed his eyes, his breathing harsh. "The scoundrel! How dare he think that he can force my daughter's hand – and all because he wants her dowry? He has brought his own poverty upon himself and yet he thinks that *she* must be the one to rescue him from it? He does not care one iota for her and seems more than happy to leave her to suffer for the rest of her days at his hand." The Duke's gaze fell to James. "I know you will not let that happen, Lord Calverton."

It took James a moment to realize what the Duke was asking him. A slight swell of joy lifted his heart, only for a frown to settle across his feature. "What if Lady Temperance is not ready to consider matrimony?"

"Speak with her," the Duke encouraged. "I will have a Special License procured in only a few days' time. It will mean I must travel to London but that is of no difficulty to me."

"But what of Lord Barlington? Even if Lord Calverton weds your daughter, he will still have his threats. He will still carry them out, I am sure of it."

James quickly shook his head. "Not if we act quickly. If the *ton* knows of Lord Barlington's impoverished state then he will be rejected there entirely. Recall that this is precisely what he does not want! I am sure that is part of the reason he did not make his way to London, for he wants to hide the truth of his situation. But if word was to spread of what he has done and the sort of gentleman he has become, then he would not be able to lift his head up in society."

"And no-one would believe a word that he says thereafter," Lord Thurston finished, as James nodded.

"It sounds like we have a plan, gentlemen, for during my visit to London for the license, I will be able to say a good many things about Lord Barlington," the Duke said, clapping one hand on James' shoulder and the other onto Lord Thurston's. "Thanks to you both, my daughter is safe."

James managed a small smile. "And so she shall always be, Your Grace. I assure you of that."

Chapter Twenty-Five

"Temperance?"

Hearing Lord Calverton's voice, Temperance turned at once and then hurried across the room towards him, her paint smeared hands outstretched. "Lord Calverton. Is there any hope?" She took in his expression, seeing the smudges of tiredness around his eyes, the seriousness etched into his face though, one his hands were holding hers tightly, he smiled.

Instantly, relief flooded through Temperance as she took in his expression. "There is hope?"

"Yes, there is," he told her, quietly. "My dear Temperance, your father, Lord Thurston and I found ourselves in company with Lord Barlington last evening, though he was too much in his cups to recognise us. He said a great deal – words that I will not bring myself to repeat here – but it was enough. Your father understands everything now, as do Lord Thurston and myself." His fingers tightened on hers again. "Would you truly have given up your freedom – your life – for me?"

She nodded. "I could not have you injured," she answered, her voice a little hoarse. "I wanted to do nothing other than protect you. To protect *all* of you."

"But you would have lost so much," he said, looking straight down at her, his eyes searching hers. "You would have given up your whole life."

With a small, soft smile, Temperance pressed her fingers through his. "It would have been worth it to know that everyone I cared for, everyone I loved, was safe."

Lord Calverton's eyebrows lifted a little and Temperance's heart leapt, realizing what it was she had said. Did she love Lord Calverton? Yes, she cared for him and certainly, the affection within her heart had grown significantly these last few days... but did that mean she loved him?

"You do really care for me, do you not?" he asked, his voice filled with a tenderness which made her blush.

"Yes," she answered, not willing to hold the truth back from him. "Yes, I do."

Lord Calverton let out a long, slow breath though he smiled at her thereafter, making her realize that he was very glad indeed to hear those words from her lips.

"You cannot know how glad I am to hear that," he murmured, quietly. "Lady Temperance, there is something that I must ask you. You see, once your father, Lord Thurston and I stood outside together, your father suggested that there was only one way to make certain that Lord Barlington could never force your hand in such a way again. It is a suggestion which may come as something of a surprise to you, but I can assure you that my own heart is more than contented with the idea."

A flickering frown went across Temperance's forehead. "What do you mean?"

Lord Calverton looked away, licking his lips. "Well," he began, slowly, turning his gaze back towards her, "if we were to… and that is not to say that I do not *want* to, for the truth is, I want this very much and I know that it is rather sudden but all the same, I – " He came to a sudden stop, his lips bunching as he gazed back at her. "Temperance," he said, his voice now steady. "I want to marry you."

It was as though all of the air from the room had been sucked out in one go, leaving her feeling a little light-headed and breathless. Her hands tightened on his, her eyes wide as shock lodged in her chest.

"I know that it is sudden, that it is a great shock," Lord Calverton continued, speaking a little more quickly now, "but it is a way to save you from all that Lord Barlington has threatened. But more than that, Temperance, it is because I *want* to do this that I bring the proposal to you. I truly do desire to have you as my wife. I think that you are the most beautiful, the most delightful, the most incredible young lady and to have been given the opportunity to meet you, to know you and to fall in love with you is a joy that I am truly grateful for." He took another step closer to her, so there was barely an inch between them. "Temperance, I want nothing more than to heal the pain that Lord Barlington has caused you. I want to be able to take all the darkness he has left you with and throw it aside, filling that space in your heart with light instead. I want to give you the life and the future that you deserve, to offer you companionship, love and happiness in a life shared together. I want to do all of this for you, Temperance, because I care for you. I am falling in love with you and to have you as my wife would be a blessing beyond measure."

Temperance let out a ragged gasp, only for Lord Calverton's eyes to flare, perhaps concerned that she was much too shocked, too overwhelmed to respond. He released her hands and made to take a step back, perhaps worried that she was going to refuse him, only for Temperance to throw her arms around his neck.

Her heart was screaming with joy, tears of happiness beginning to drip down her cheeks. She let out a half laugh, half sob as his arms wrapped tightly around her waist, pulling her close to him.

"You are not upset about my question, are you?" he murmured in her ear, sounding relieved. "I must hope that this means you are going to accept?"

"Of *course* I am going to accept!" She cried, unable to pull herself away from him for fear that her heart would completely and utterly explode should she look into his eyes. "I cannot quite believe that you have asked me to marry you! I did not think that I would ever be given such an opportunity again – and certainly not from someone who cares for me in the same way as I care for them!"

"And I thought you were more than contented as a spinster," he told her, making her laugh as she leaned back just a little, though she did not loosen her arms from around his neck. "I was afraid that you might reject me for your life here is just as you like it."

Temperance shook her head. "No, you misunderstood me when I spoke. It is not that I was contented as I was for I have been full of sadness and grief, though I have found a solace here which has been a great benefit to me. I spoke so because I did not believe for a single moment that a gentleman might ever look at me in such a way."

Lord Calverton tilted his head. "Because of your scar?"

She nodded. "Lord Barlington rejected me because of it. He told me, in no uncertain terms, that I was flawed, damaged and broken and he could never consider having such a young lady on his arm as his wife. Therefore, I believed that all gentlemen would feel the same way about someone who is not perfect, as they ought to be."

With a gentle hand, Lord Calverton ran one finger lightly down her scar, his eyes going to it. Temperance did not feel a single iota of fear, did not pull her face away from him as he did so. Nor did she feel any shame as his eyes returned to hers. Lord Calverton knew everything about what had happened, he looked at her scar but he did not really *see* it, not in the way that Lord Barlington and even her own family did.

"I think that you are beautiful." His hand ran down to the curve of her throat, leaving sparks behind his fingers as he let his touch run down her shoulder and then all the way down her arm to capture her hand again. "Your eyes capture my very soul. Your lips beg for me to kiss them. The sweetness of your smile thrills me. The nearness of you sets my whole being aflame."

She trembled lightly at the fervency of his words.

"I want to marry you so that I can have the privilege of calling you my wife for the rest of my days," he finished, making her heart sing. "You will not have to give up your life and your future for the wickedness of one supposed gentleman. You will have happiness and love and joy, Temperance. I swear that to you."

"Then how could I do anything other than accept?" she whispered, her heart so full, she could barely contain the ecstasy which filled her. "Oh, Calverton, you have answered my wildest dreams – dreams I did not know I could even permit myself to have! Yes, I will marry you. I will marry you this day if you can manage it!"

He laughed and, catching her up in his arms again, kissed her gently. She responded at once, her arms tight around his neck, her fingers threading through his hair. It was a soft, sweet kiss but there were still traces of heat at the edges, sending a gentle trembling through her.

"I presume that my niece has agreed then?"

Temperance broke from Lord Calverton's kiss with a start, fire reaching up to burn in her cheeks as her aunt smiled at her from the doorway.

"Your father told me everything before he quit the house," she said, her eyes holding lingering tears. "I cannot believe that you would be so generous as to give yourself up to save everyone else – but then again, given that I know your sweet nature and gentle character, I should not be surprised." She came a little further into the room. "Your father has taken your mother with him to fetch a Special License. You will be able to marry within the week."

"He has gone to London?" Temperance blinked quickly. "But surely a Common License would have done just as well, though we might have had to wait a few days longer?"

Lord Calverton smiled. "Ah, but in going to London, your father is able to make a few particular remarks to a few particular people." His smile grew as Temperance gazed at him, not understanding. "Lord Barlington has hidden himself from London because he does not want anyone to know of his impoverished state. Your father, in making his way there, will have opportunity to tell everyone what he knows of Lord Barlington now, as well as given the *ton* the promise that his words can be verified by Lord Thurston, by another gentleman by the name of Sir Jeffries and by myself. So, when the time comes for Lord Barlington to understand that you and I are already wed and he cannot gain what he desires, he will, no doubt, state that he will carry out what he has already threatened."

"But by that time, the *ton* will already have heard everything that the Duke of Danfield has said and, no doubt, some creditors might appear also, confirming what has been said of Lord Barlington's impoverished state," her aunt finished. "He can do and say all that he wants, but the majority of the *ton* will not believe him."

Temperance let out a breath, warmth enveloping her. "And so we will be safe."

"Yes, my darling," Lord Calverton murmured, coming close to her again despite her aunt's presence. "We will be safe, forever."

She turned to him, her eyes alight with happiness, their fingers intertwining again. "Then all we have to do is wait."

"Yes, you do," her aunt stated, breaking Temperance's intimate moment with her betrothed apart. "But I am still here to be your chaperone, my dear!" She laughed as Temperance's expression grew a little frustrated. "Though I have some further news for you, which I think will lift your spirits even more."

"Oh?"

Lady Hartford smiled. "Your father took your mother with him, as I told you. However, he assured me that by the time they returned, your mother would understand completely all that has taken place and would be, as he insisted, more than glad at the marriage which is to take place." Her expression softened. "I do not think for a moment that your mother meant any ill in pushing you towards Lord Barlington, my dear. I think that she wanted her daughter to marry the very highest title that could be reached and she did not have any knowledge of Lord Barlington's true character."

Temperance nodded. "I understand that, Aunt, and I am glad to hear that my mother might return with a happier countenance." She recalled how she had been forced to stay in company with Lord Barlington, forced into the conversation where she had been threatened with such awful things if she did not do as was asked. She did not believe for a moment that her mother would ever have wanted that for her.

"What if Lord Barlington returns to the house?" Lord Calverton asked, looking to Lady Hartford. "We must wait until the Duke returns with the Special License which will be some days, but what shall we do if he comes to call, if he demands to see Temperance?"

Lady Hartford shrugged. "I will simply make the excuse that Temperance is unwell and cannot have company. Believe me, Lord Calverton, I can make certain that he does not set foot into this house!"

"Though that does mean that you will have to remain indoors until your father returns, Temperance," Lord Calverton said, looking back at her. "I know how much you love walking along the cliffs and the shoreline. Will you be able to refrain from such a thing?"

She laughed, an idea for a painting coming to her. She knew exactly what she could do during these few days. She adored painting the outside landscapes, she thought there was nothing better than standing out at the shoreline, sketching the ever changing waves and clouds but now, standing with Lord Calverton, Temperance finally saw something even more wonderful. She had once drawn him standing on the shore, albeit without realizing what she was doing, but now she had time, opportunity and inclination to draw him just as she was. These next few days, she would think only of him, would sketch only his profile, would paint only his features. It would be her wedding gift to him – and, mayhap, she might paint him one new painting every year. That would be her way of showing her affection for him, showing him how much he had come to mean to her. In an instant, the thought of being alone with only her paints seemed an excellent one. "Yes, I think I shall be able to endure it, Lord Calverton, especially in light of what is waiting for me in only a few days' time." Her hand squeezed his. "Though will you be able to make preparations for the wedding without me? If I am to be ill, then it is not as though I can go running about the house and the grounds for fear that Lord Barlington might spy me somehow. He can be very determined when he wants and his suspicions might very well grow despite Lady Hartford's insistence that I am too unwell to see him. He is well aware that I do not want to wed him and is more than likely to see that this is an excuse."

Lord Calverton nodded. "Of course, do not fear about such things. Your aunt and I can arrange everything, I am sure." He looked to Lady Hartford who smiled her agreement. "I can hardly wait for that day, Temperance."

Sighing gently, she leaned into him again, wishing that her aunt were not present. "Nor can I, Lord Calverton. I already know that it will be the happiest day of my life."

Chapter Twenty-Six

James' heart pounded furiously as he stood at the front of the church, waiting for Lady Temperance's arrival. Unable to prevent the swirl of fear within him, afraid that something dreadful might happen still, he swallowed tightly and bounced gently on his toes. What if Lord Barlington had discovered that there was to be a wedding? What if he came to disrupt the ceremony? All had gone rather well thus far but all the same, until both he and Lady Temperance were wed, James could not help but feel a little fear.

"You need not look so concerned. Here, she is coming now."

James looked first to Lord Thurston who was standing beside him as his groomsman, only to then turn and look to the door of the church.

Lady Temperance was walking towards him, resplendent in a beautiful, cream gown which swished lightly as she walked. Her fair curls danced at her temples, her face unhidden as a beautiful smile curved her lips. She was not afraid, as he was. The sheer joy on her face made James' own heart pull free of his anxiety as he let out a long, slow breath.

Lady Temperance was to be his wife and even if Lord Barlington was to appear, he could do nothing to prevent it.

"My dear," he murmured, his voice echoing around the almost empty church despite the fact that he had kept his voice low. "How beautiful you are."

She smiled up at him, her green eyes clear though her hand still stayed on her father's arm rather than reaching for his. It was not yet time even though James yearned for her touch.

The vicar cleared his throat and, forcing his gaze away from Lady Temperance, James gave him a small nod. He was more than ready for the ceremony to begin.

Opening up his Book of Common Prayer, the vicar's eyes darted around the church, taking in the three others present: the Duchess of Danfield, Lady Thurston and Lady Hartford.

And then, he began.

"Dearly beloved, we are gathered together here in the sight of God, and in the face of this congregation, to join together this Man and this Woman in holy matrimony. It is not to be taken in hand unadvisedly, lightly, or wantonly but reverently, discreetly, advisedly, soberly, and in the fear of God; duly considering the causes for which matrimony was ordained. Therefore, if any man can show any just cause, why they may not lawfully be joined together, let him now speak, or else hereafter forever hold his peace."

James smiled at Lady Temperance as the quiet few moments continued to dance around them. There was no-one to protest and yet, the vicar continued to wait. Everything had to be done correctly, despite how desperate James was for the ceremony to continue.

After what felt like an age, the vicar then turned his attention back towards James and Lady Temperance, a light smile on his lips. "I charge you both, as you will answer at the dreadful day of judgment when the secrets of all hearts shall be disclosed, that if either of you know any impediment, why you may not be lawfully joined together in matrimony, you do now confess it."

Again, James shared a glance with Lady Temperance, seeing the gentle smile on her lips as she held his gaze for another moment. No, he wanted to shout, there is no impediment! All he wanted was to have his moment to declare his love and devotion to Lady Temperance and thus far, it seemed an age in coming.

"Very well." The vicar paused again, then looked at James, a seriousness in his expression. "James, Earl of Calverton will you have this woman as your wedded wife, to live together after God's ordinance in the holy estate of matrimony? Will you love her, comfort her, honour, and keep her in sickness and in health; and, forsaking all other, keep only unto her, so long as you both shall live?"

"I will." The words could not have been spoken more quickly and James' heart lifted with happiness as Lady Temperance smiled up at him.

"Then Lady Temperance?" Again the vicar paused as though Lady Temperance might wish to take in the solemnity of the moment. "Lady Temperance, will you have this man as your wedded husband, to live together after God's ordinance in the holy estate of matrimony? Will you obey him, and serve him, love, honour, and keep him in sickness and in health; and, forsaking all other, keep only unto him, so long as you both shall live?

"I will." Her voice was soft but the promise sincere and despite the importance of the moment, James could not help but smile broadly. How much he wanted to take her hand! How much he desired to have her near him!

He did not have to wait much longer. With a nod, the vicar then turned to the Duke of Danfield, who had been standing solemnly beside his daughter since the very beginning of the ceremony.

"Who gives this woman to be married to this man?"

"I do." The Duke took a step closer, with his daughter beside him. The vicar smiled briefly, then took Lady Temperance's hand and, after a moment, turned towards James.

He was more than ready. Reaching out, he took Lady Temperance's hand in his own, a thrill racing up his arm and into his heart as she finally not only stood near him but looked up into his eyes, her hand in his own.

"Then, Lord Calverton, might you repeat these words?"

James nodded and did as he was asked. "I, James, the Earl of Calverton take you Lady Temperance to be my wedded wife, to have and to hold from this day forward, for better for worse, for richer for poorer, in sickness and in health, to love and to cherish, till death us do part, according to God's holy ordinance."

Tears came into Lady Temperance's eyes as she then took her turn, repeating the words after the vicar. "I, Lady Temperance take you James, the Earl of Calverton to be my wedded Husband, to have and to hold from this day forward, for better for worse, for richer for poorer, in sickness and in health, to love, cherish, and to obey, till death us do part, according to God's holy ordinance."

James pressed her hand gently, seeing how she blinked back the tears of happiness.

"Lord Thurston?"

After a moment, Lord Thurston handed the vicar a small, gold ring, having it then placed on the Bible, the vicar held out it him. With a broad smile, James took it from him and taking Lady Temperance's hand, held it to her finger.

"Lord Calverton, speak these words after me," the vicar intoned, as James nodded. Lady Temperance looked into his eyes, her lips curved softly and James' heart exploded with all the love he felt for her.

"With this ring, I thee wed. With my body, I thee worship, and with all my worldly goods, I thee endow."

The vicar nodded. "In the Name of the Father, and of the Son, and of the Holy Ghost."

At that, James pushed the ring onto Lady Temperance's finger and then pressed her hand again with his. He took in a deep breath and then let it out again, overjoyed at this wondrous moment which was so near to completion.

The vicar set his hand over their joined ones and then looked out at the sparse congregation. "Those whom God hath joined together let no man put asunder. For as much as James, the Earl of Calverton and Lady Temperance have consented together in holy wedlock and have witnessed the same before God and this company, and thereto have given and pledged their troth to each other and have declared the same by giving and receiving of a ring and by joining of hands; I pronounce that they be Man and Wife together, In the Name of the Father, and of the Son, and of the Holy Ghost. Amen."

James turned, taking Lady Temperance with him as they both knelt down, ready to receive the final blessing. His heart was pounding, relief and joy twining together and rushing through his veins as the vicar prayed over them both.

"May God the Father, God the Son, God the Holy Ghost, bless, preserve, and keep you. May the Lord mercifully with his favour look upon you; and so fill you with all spiritual benediction and grace, that you may so live together in this life, that in the world to come you may have life everlasting. Amen."

"Amen," James murmured, hearing Lady Temperance say the very same thing. He turned to look at her and saw one single tear drip to her cheek, though her smile was dazzling. Did she too feel the very same delight that he did? Was she too just as relieved, just as contented as he? The next few minutes passed by with great speed as the marriage lines were signed and, thereafter, James looked down into his bride's face and, after a moment, caught her up in his arms. Normally such a thing would not have been permitted at a wedding service but, given that there were so few guests and the church such a small one, James did not care.

"My hearty congratulations!" Lord Thurston clapped James on the back as he released Lady Temperance, though caught her hand immediately thereafter. "This brings us all such great joy."

In an instant, Lady Thurston, the Duchess of Danfield and Lady Hartford surrounded them both, each exclaiming with great joy and with all the ladies taking out their handkerchiefs to wipe away lingering tears. James could not help but beam with pride and delight, Lady Temperance's hand on his arm – only for a loud exclamation to interrupt them all.

"What is the meaning of this?"

James reached across and kept Lady Temperance's hand on his arm, feeling her jump in surprise as Lord Barlington strode into the church, his face a picture of anger. His brows were low over his eyes, his gaze sharp and angry, his hands curling up into tight fists.

"*I* am engaged to Lady Temperance," he hissed, pointing one hand at Lady Temperance. "*We* are to be wed! This is nothing but a sham!"

The vicar cleared his throat. "I was unaware of – "

"That is because this man is telling you nothing but lies," the Duke interrupted calmly, turning to face the vicar. "You did as you were expected to do and there was no-one to protest. As Lady Temperance's father, I can assure you that I have never given consent to my daughter being wed to Lord Barlington. Besides which, you saw the license yourself, did you not?"

"Yes, I did." The vicar, said clearly relieved, then chose to step away, leaving them all to face Lord Barlington without his presence.

James did nothing but smile as Lord Barlington's angry gaze turned towards him, his hands now planted at his waist as he glared at him.

"There is no reason for you to be here, Lord Barlington," the Duke said, firmly. "We do not desire your presence."

"*I* am engaged to Lady Temperance!" Lord Barlington exclaimed again, only for the Duke to take a step forward.

"No, you are not," he stated, firmly. "You did not come to seek my consent and I did not give it. Instead, you thought to threaten my daughter with horrific consequences if she did not do as you asked."

Lord Barlington's mouth fell open, his eyes flaring wide and for a moment, James thought that the man might protest, that he might state he had done nothing but instead, he simply shrugged.

"I have married Lady Temperance and am now her husband," James told Lord Barlington, seeing the man scowl darkly.

"And before you begin to even think that you will bring about the consequences you threatened, might I tell you that the Duke of Danfield himself has only recently returned from London!"

Lord Barlington's eyes flicked to the Duke of Danfield.

"Hearing you speak of my daughter and the cruelty you planned to inflict upon her changed my opinion of you very quickly, Lord Barlington," the Duke said, crisply. "Sir Jeffries informed us of your impoverished state and you, in your drunkenness, confirmed it all. So, given that I thought to go to London to get the Special License, I decided that I would, at the same time, inform the *ton* about your present new situation. I can tell you that there were those within the *ton* who were very interested indeed to hear about such things. I also had the pleasure in telling them where you resided at present and you may soon find yourself discovered, Lord Barlington. You may have unexpected guests, each seeking out what you owe them."

James smiled grimly as Lord Barlington took a small step back, shock beginning to drain away his dark, angry expression.

"You will never have my daughter's hand." This time, it was the Duchess who spoke, her words practically hissing out of her. "Never. I believed you when you told me how much you regretted ending the engagement, but I see now that it was nothing more than greed on your part. You wanted to take Temperance's dowry and her yearly income and save yourself from your circumstances – circumstances which you have brought upon yourself! I caused my daughter a great deal of pain because of your words and have nothing but regret."

"You did not know, Mama," Temperance said softly, as James offered the Duchess a small smile. "There is nothing either myself or my husband hold against you."

At the name, 'husband', James' heart leapt furiously and he smiled, looking down at his bride.

"This is a day of joy," he said, quietly. "Lord Barlington, your presence is no longer required here." He looked back at the gentleman, then cut through the air between them with one hand, dismissing him. "There is nothing more you can say or do in this situation. You shall not have what you hoped for, what you *schemed* for. Good day, Lord Barlington. If you will excuse me, I fully intend to take my bride back to my manor so we might begin our life together."

Without another word, James walked past Lord Barlington, his wife on his arm, and made his way out of the church. Once outside, he turned, gathered Lady Temperance in his arms and, without hesitation, kissed her.

All the world fell away as he held her close. Everything that had hindered, everything that had pulled them back was gone. Lord Barlington had no hold on them any longer, no threats of his could stand. All there was now was their bright, golden future that was waiting for them.

"I love you, Temperance," he murmured, his words brushing at her lips. "We are man and wife now, are we not?"

She giggled, free from the shadows Lord Barlington had cast over them both. "Yes, Calverton, I believe we are." With her hands, she framed his face, her eyes melding to his. "And I love you too."

Epilogue

"Temperance? Where are you?"

Temperance smiled to herself, squinting at her canvas before she turned her head to greet her husband as he walked into the room. He paused for a moment, his eyes going over the scene before him.

"I am afraid that the twins thought they might help me with my painting this afternoon," she told him, giggling as the two twins both looked up at once, smiles of adoration spreading across their faces as they saw their father. They both rushed towards Lord Calverton, their paint-smeared hands reaching out to him.

"Wait a moment, wait a moment!" she cried, as Lord Calverton laughed and dodged his two children with ease, coming across the room to join her. "Here, now. Let the nursemaid clean your hands and then you can have Papa pick you up and whirl you around the room as he always does." She smiled at them both as the nursemaid quickly came to lead the children from the room, promising that they would return very quickly once their hands were clean.

"Our two boys must be the most beautiful of all children, I think," Lord Calverton murmured, his arms going about her waist as Temperance melted into him. "You have given me so many blessings, Temperance."

"As I have been blessed by you," she answered, reaching up to kiss him. "It has almost been two years since we were wed, has it not?"

His eyes glinted. "It has been."

"Then I have a gift for you."

Lord Calverton lifted an eyebrow. "A gift?"

She nodded. "On the day of our wedding, I gave you a painting of a gentleman walking on the beach, do you recall?"

Lord Calverton's eyes lit up. "I do. Of course I do. It was the most beautiful painting."

"I have something more to show you," she said, taking him by the hand and walking over to the easel. "It is still not quite dry but it is finished."

She watched his eyes as he took in the scene. It brought her such joy to see how happy such a small thing made him. Looking back at the painting, she smiled and tilted her head, seeing the waves and the shore that were so familiar to her. There, standing on the shoreline, she had painted a family of four. She and Lord Calverton stood together, holding one of the twins each by the hand. There was joy on each face, a love which she had tried to paint into each of their eyes – and as Lord Calverton looked back at her, Temperance knew that he felt it.

"I do not know what to say." His voice was a little hoarse, his eyes searching hers. "You have such a gift, Temperance and you use that gift to bless others. I do not know what to say to this, other than thank you. It is so incredibly beautiful, painting us all in the very place which has become our home." He swallowed hard and then looked back at it. "I do not regret deciding to make this estate my primary residence because it is here that I have found myself happy. Though, that is only because you are here with me, Temperance." He turned to her again, his smile growing as he slipped his arms around her waist. "You would make me happy no matter where we lived. Being with you, being beside you and seeing you smile make every day bright."

Temperance sighed contentedly, reaching for him as her heart flooded with a fresh surge of love. "You speak of my own heart, Calverton," she answered him, as his hands pulled her tighter against him. "As much as I love this place, as much as I love the wildness of the sea, of the waves and the beauty of the rugged landscape, I would not be contented were you not here to share it all with me."

"And we have so much still to share," he murmured, beginning to lower his head as excitement curled in Temperance's stomach. "I love you, Temperance and I swear to you, I always shall."

The End

Printed in Great Britain
by Amazon